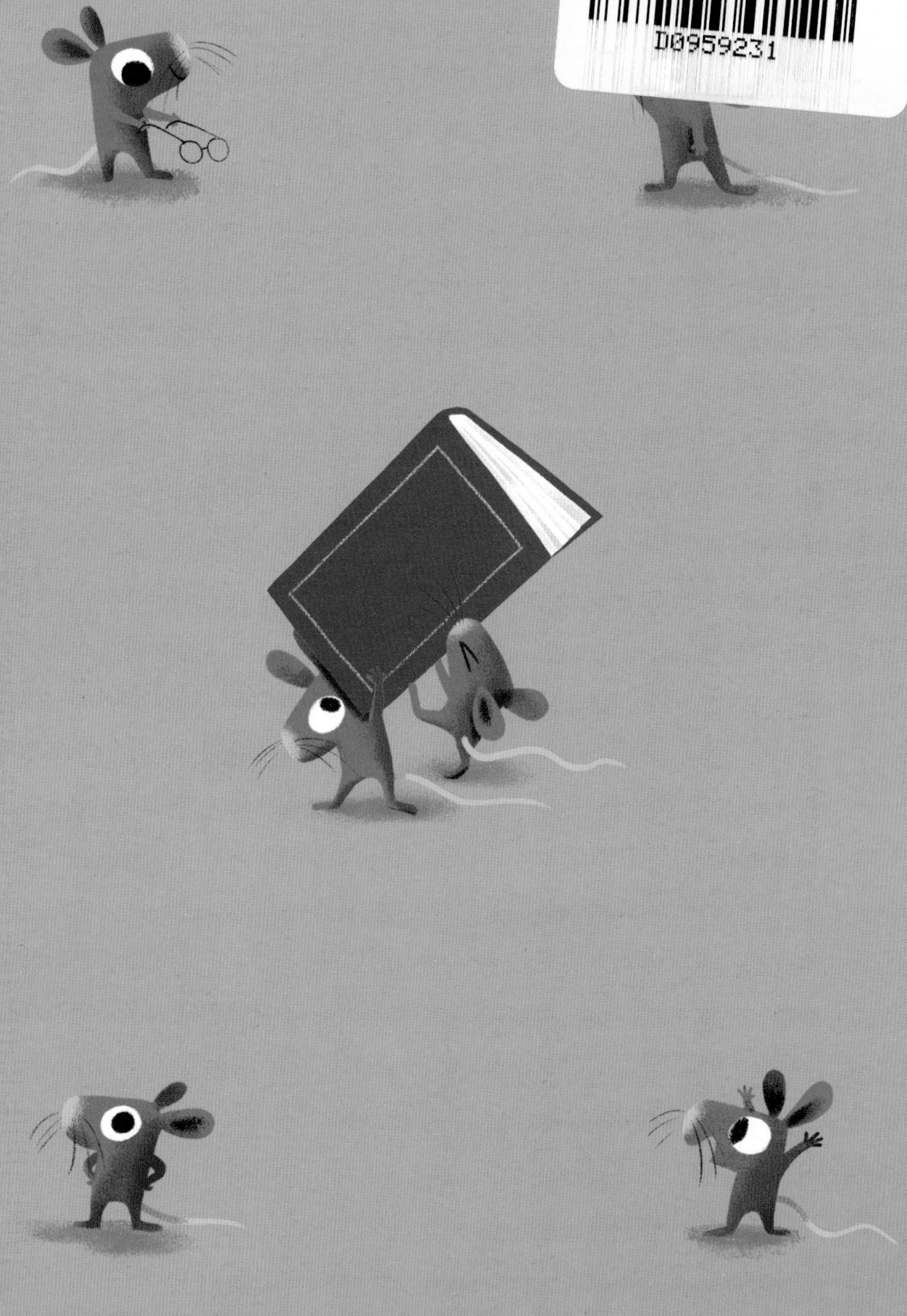

Also look for:

BOBO AND PUP-PUP: WE LOVE BUBBLES!

BOBO AND PUP-PUP: LET'S MAKE CAKE!

BOBO AND PUP-PUP: HATCH AN EGG
(Coming in January 2023)

BOBO and PUP-PUP

THE FUNNY BOOK

by Vikram Madan

illustrated by Nicola Slater

A STEPPING STONE BOOK™

Random House 🏠 New York

For Ashish, for all the times our younger selves
argued over who would read the new book first
—V.M.

To Leo and Finn
—N.S.

Text copyright © 2022 by Vikram Madan
Cover art and interior illustrations copyright © 2022 by Nicola Slater

All rights reserved. Published in the United States by Random House Children's Books,
a division of Penguin Random House LLC, New York.

Random House and the colophon are registered trademarks and A Stepping Stone Book
and the colophon are trademarks of Penguin Random House LLC.
RH Graphic with the book design is a trademark of Penguin Random House LLC.

Visit us on the Web!
rhcbooks.com

Educators and librarians, for a variety of teaching tools, visit us at RHTeachersLibrarians.com

Library of Congress Cataloging-in-Publication Data is available upon request.
ISBN 978-0-593-56280-2 (hardcover) | ISBN 978-0-593-56281-9 (library binding) |
ISBN 978-0-593-56282-6 (ebook)

MANUFACTURED IN CHINA
10 9 8 7 6 5 4 3 2 1
First Edition

Contents

Chapter 1
So Funny!

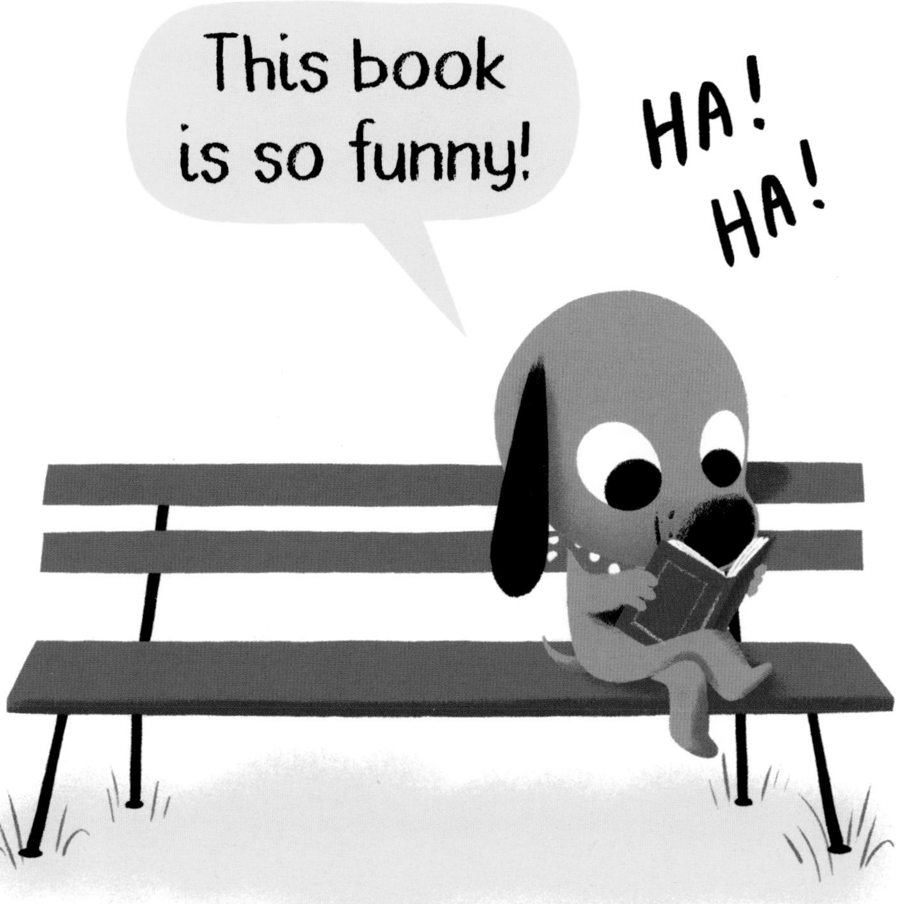
This book is so funny!
HA! HA!

Hi, Pup-Pup!
What are you
reading?

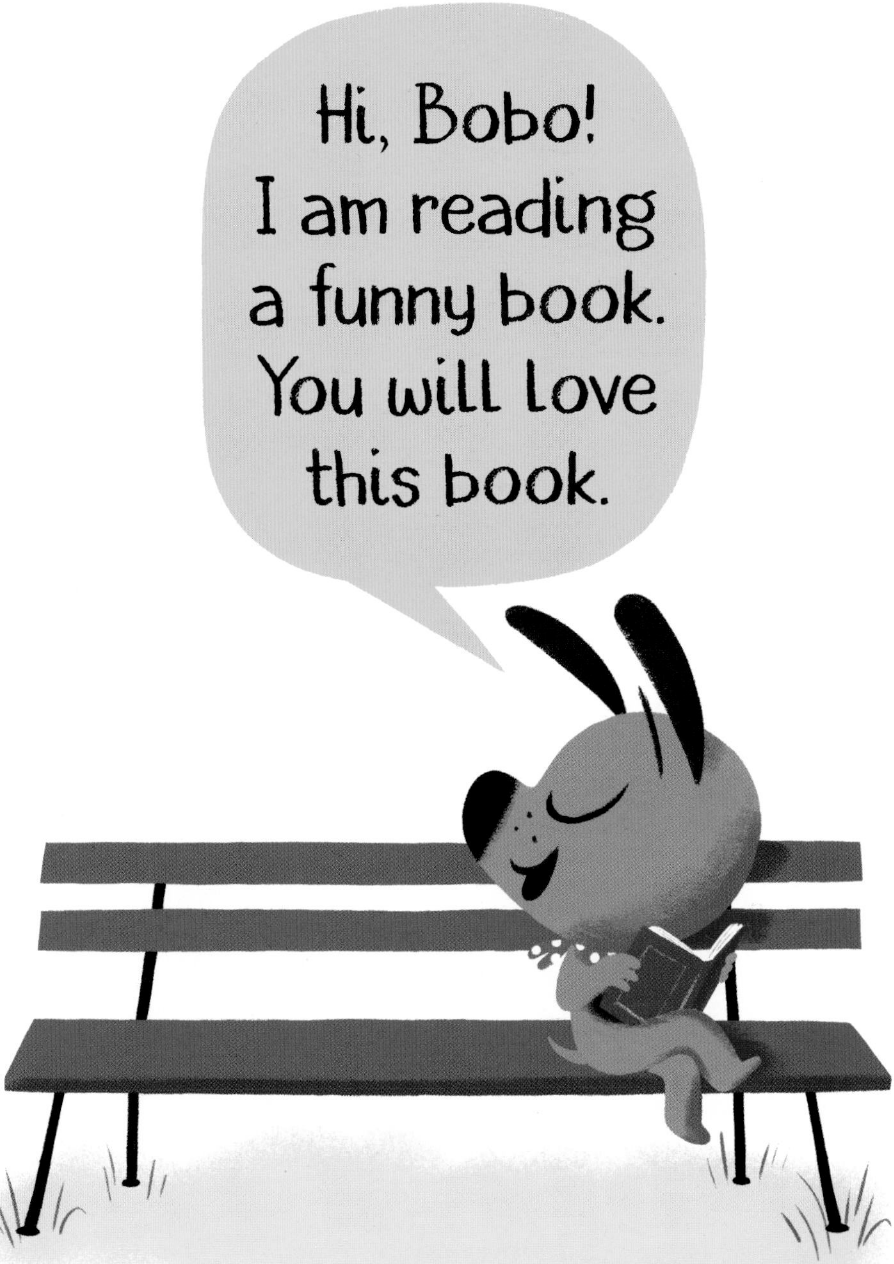
Hi, Bobo!
I am reading
a funny book.
You will love
this book.

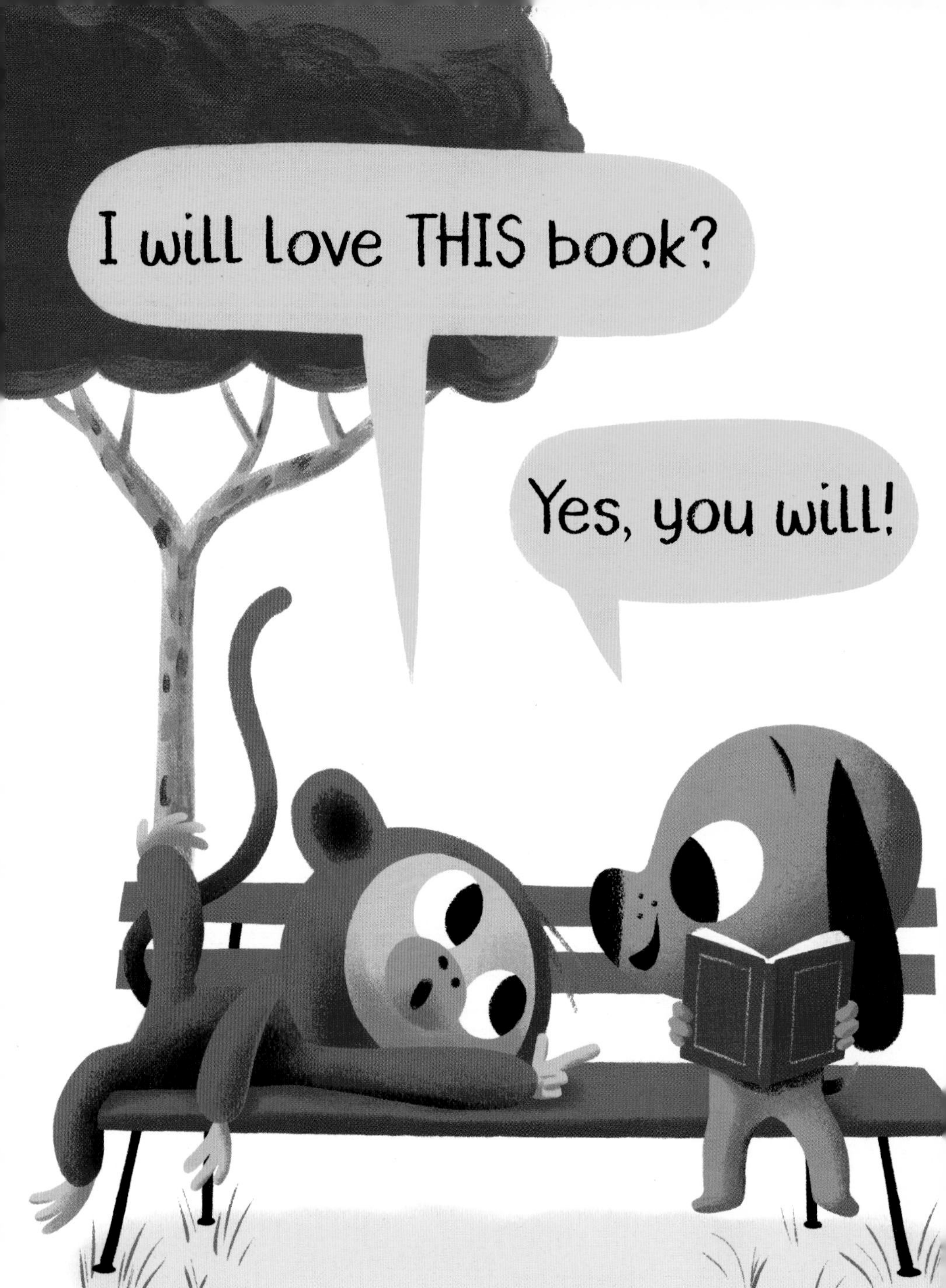
I will love THIS book?
Yes, you will!

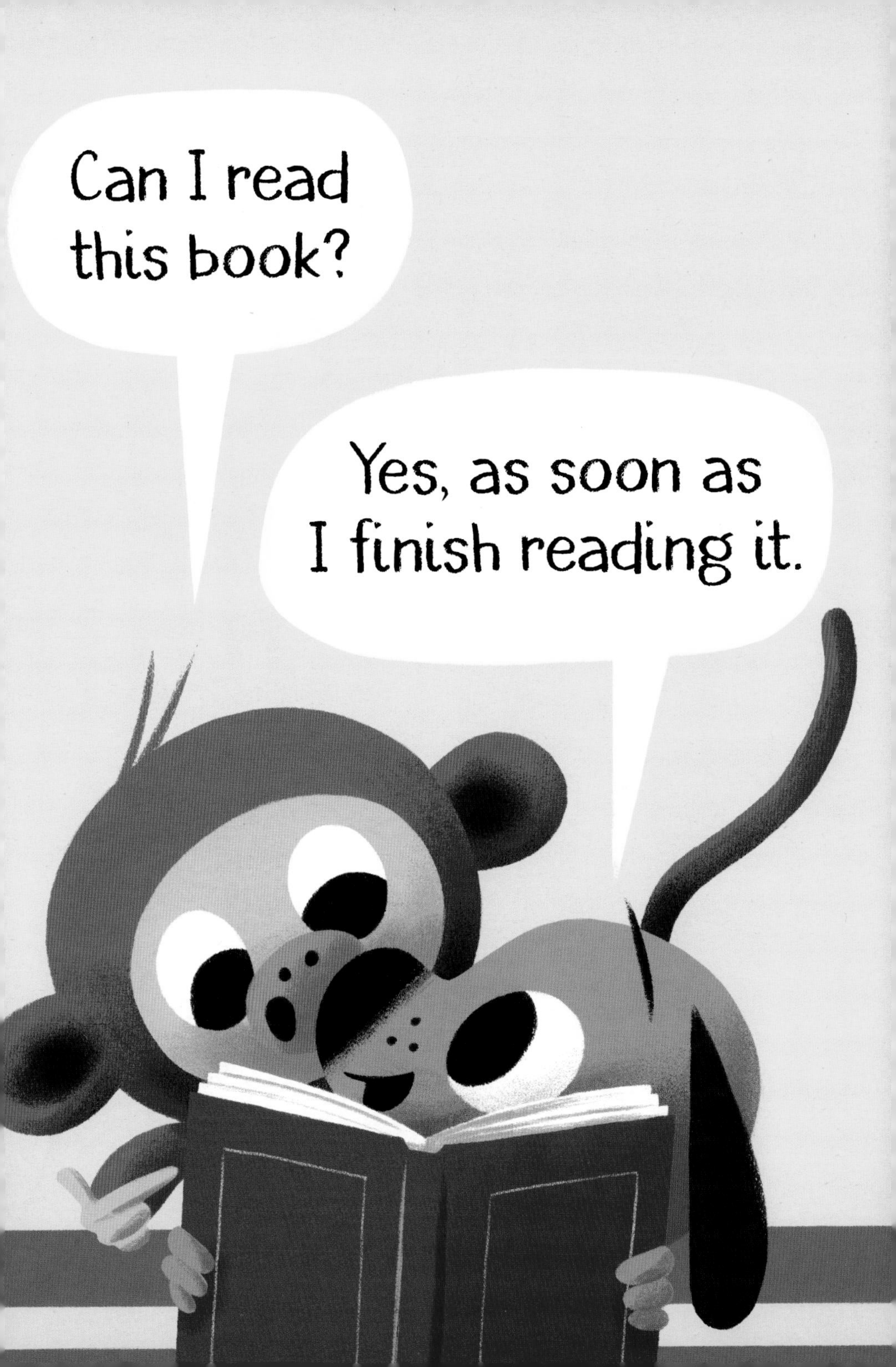
Can I read this book?
Yes, as soon as I finish reading it.

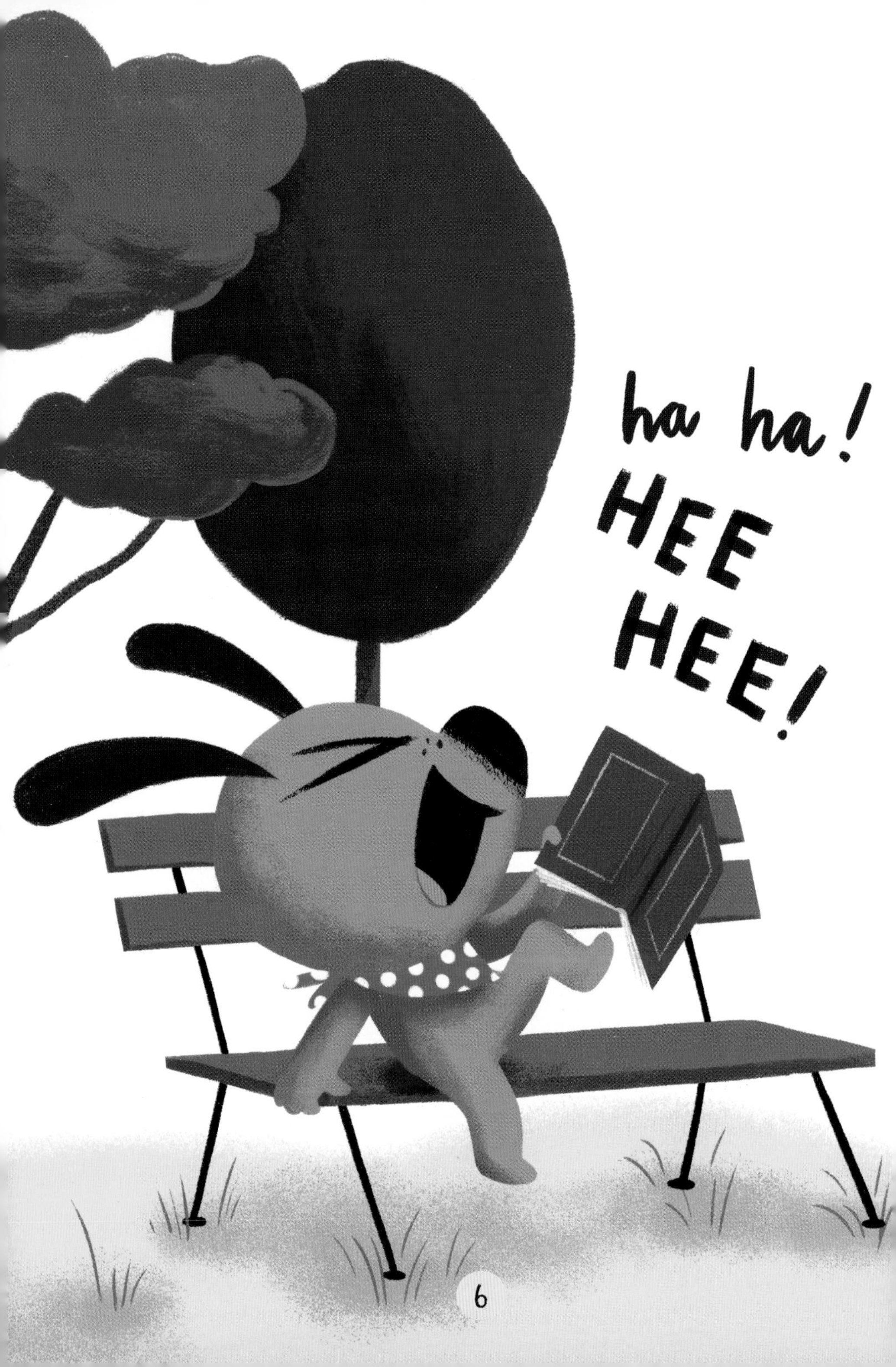
ha ha!
HEE HEE!

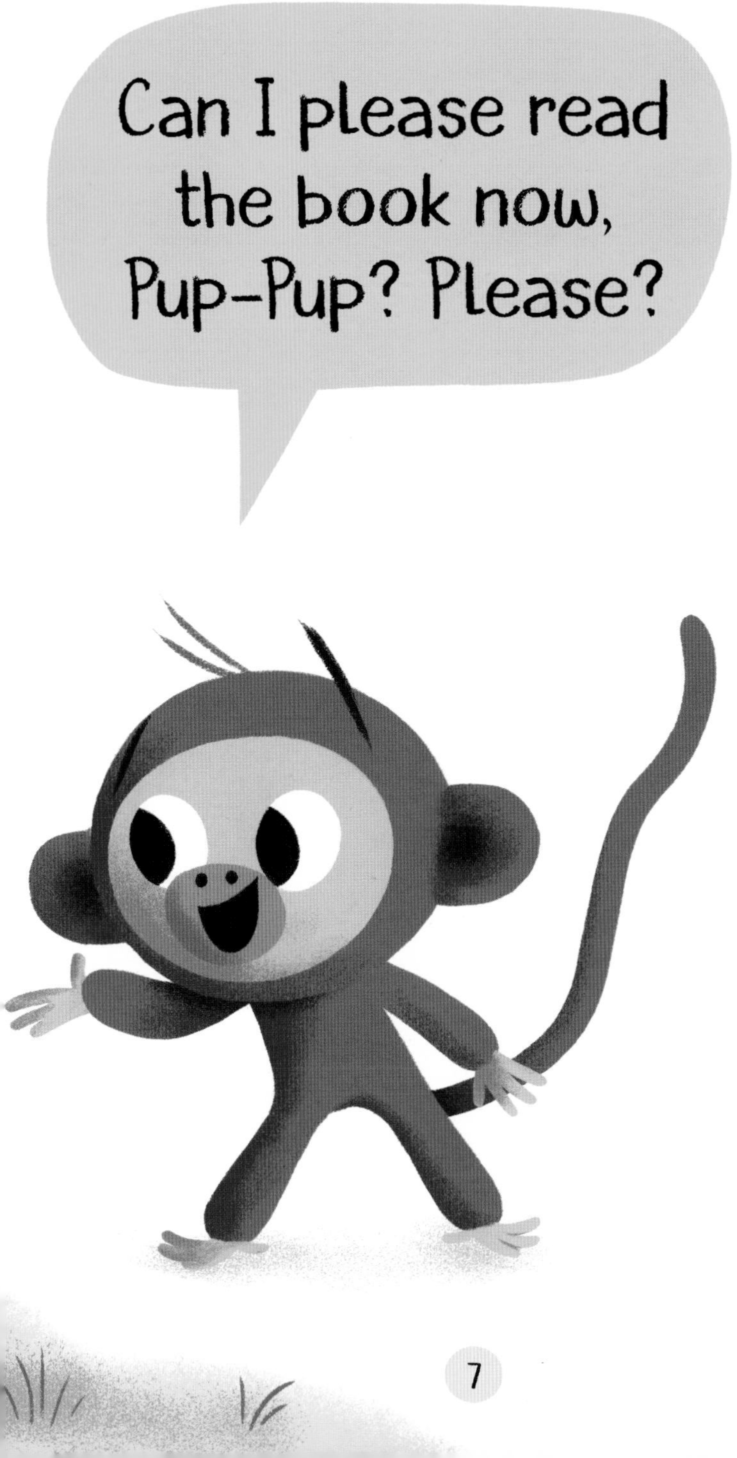
Can I please read the book now, Pup-Pup? Please?

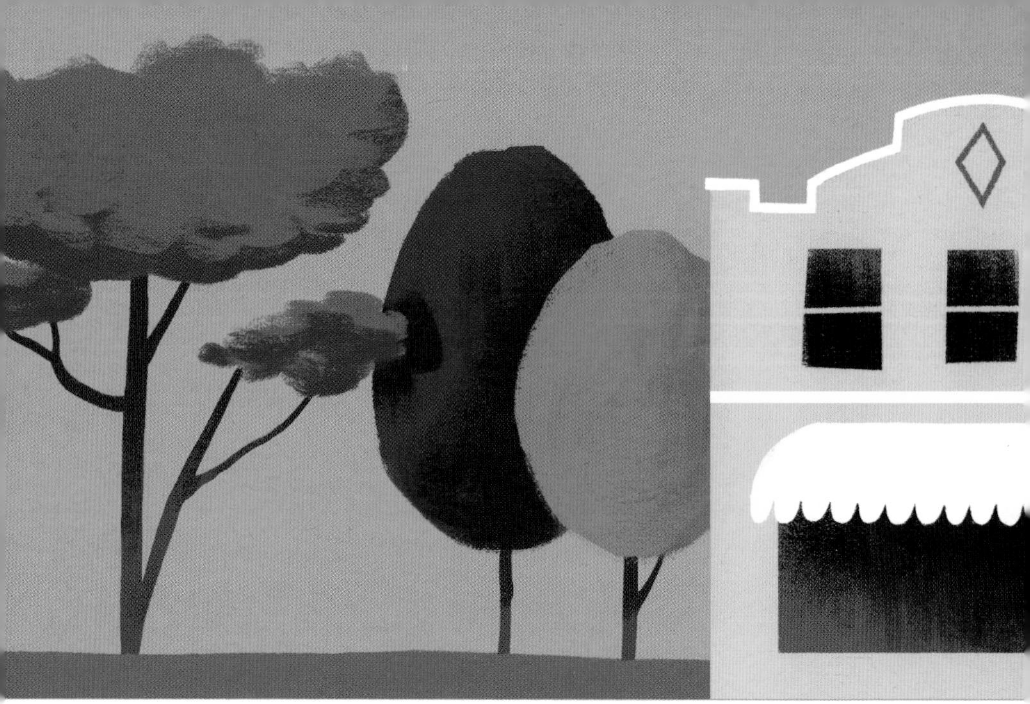

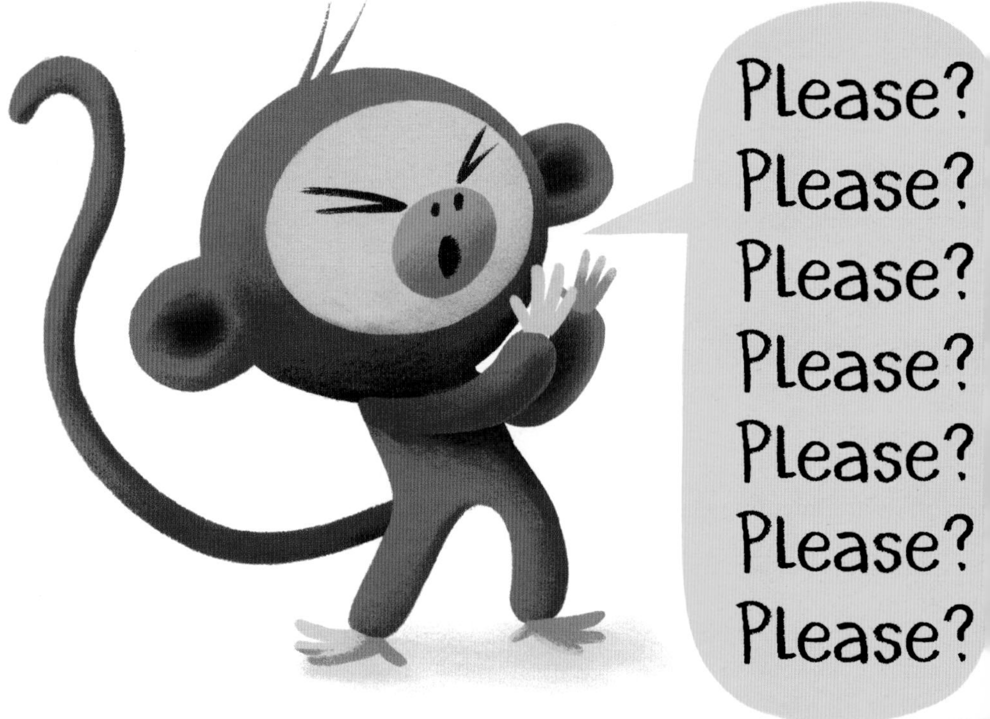
Please?
Please?
Please?
Please?
Please?
Please?
Please?

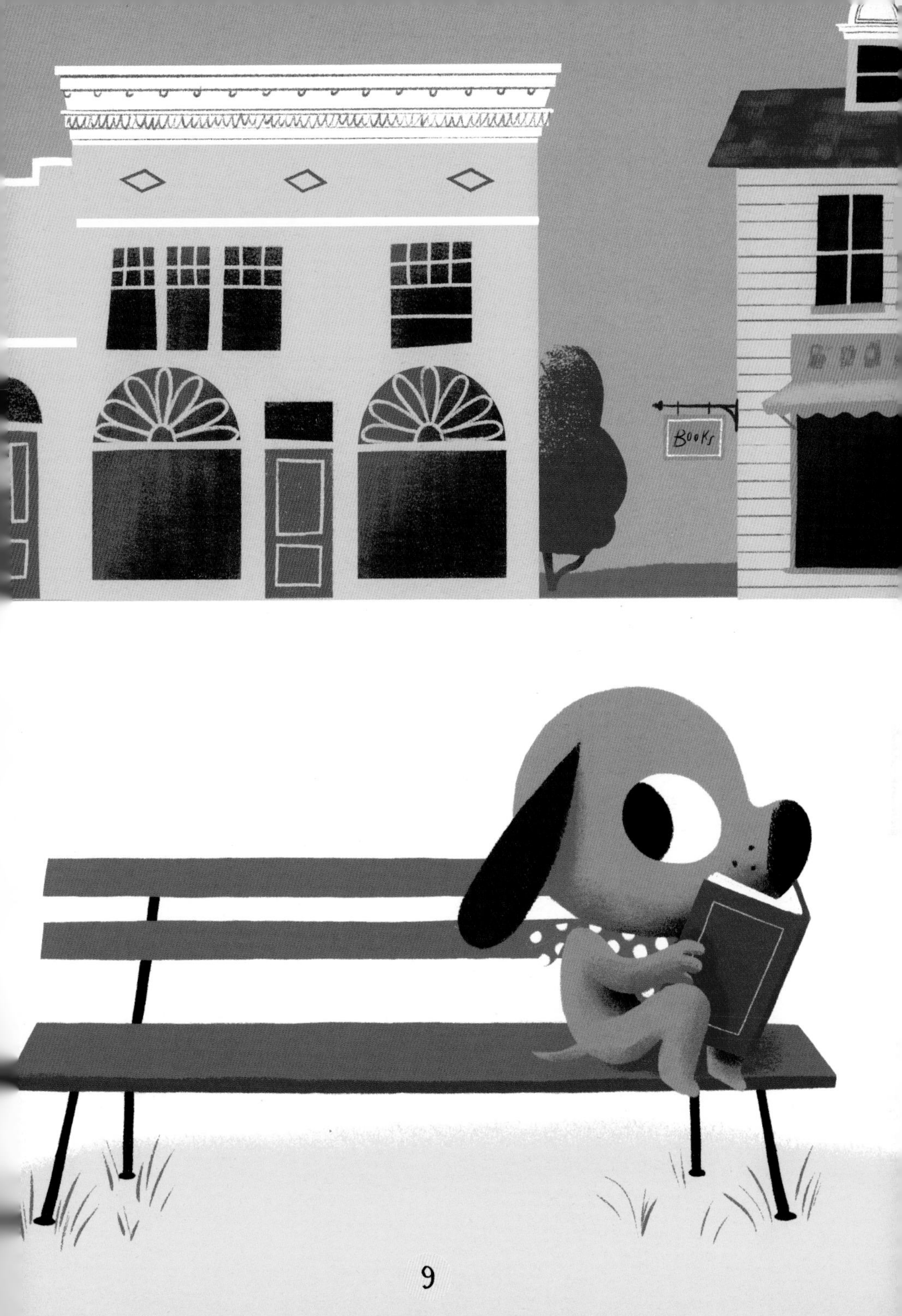
Books

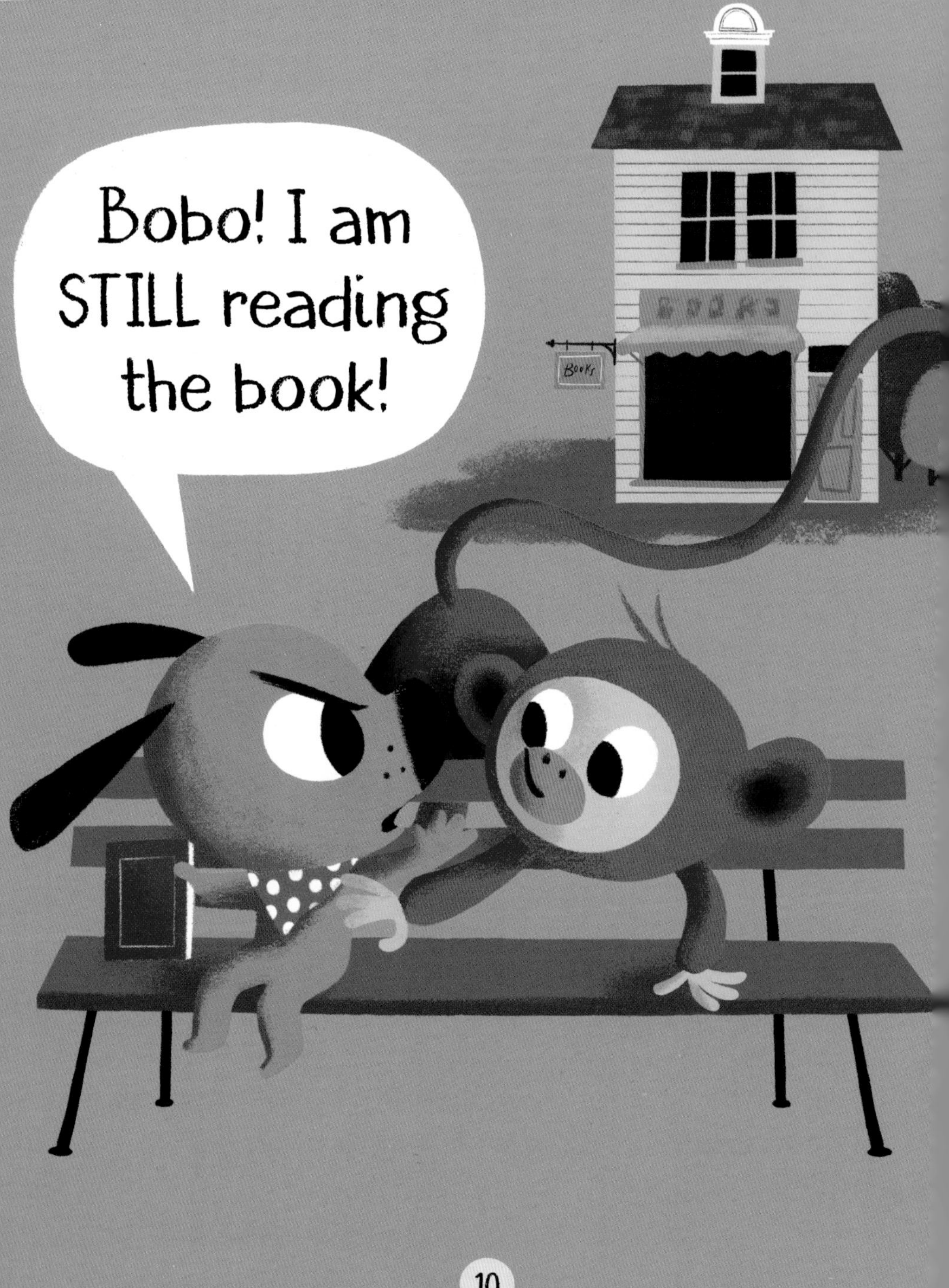
Bobo! I am STILL reading the book!

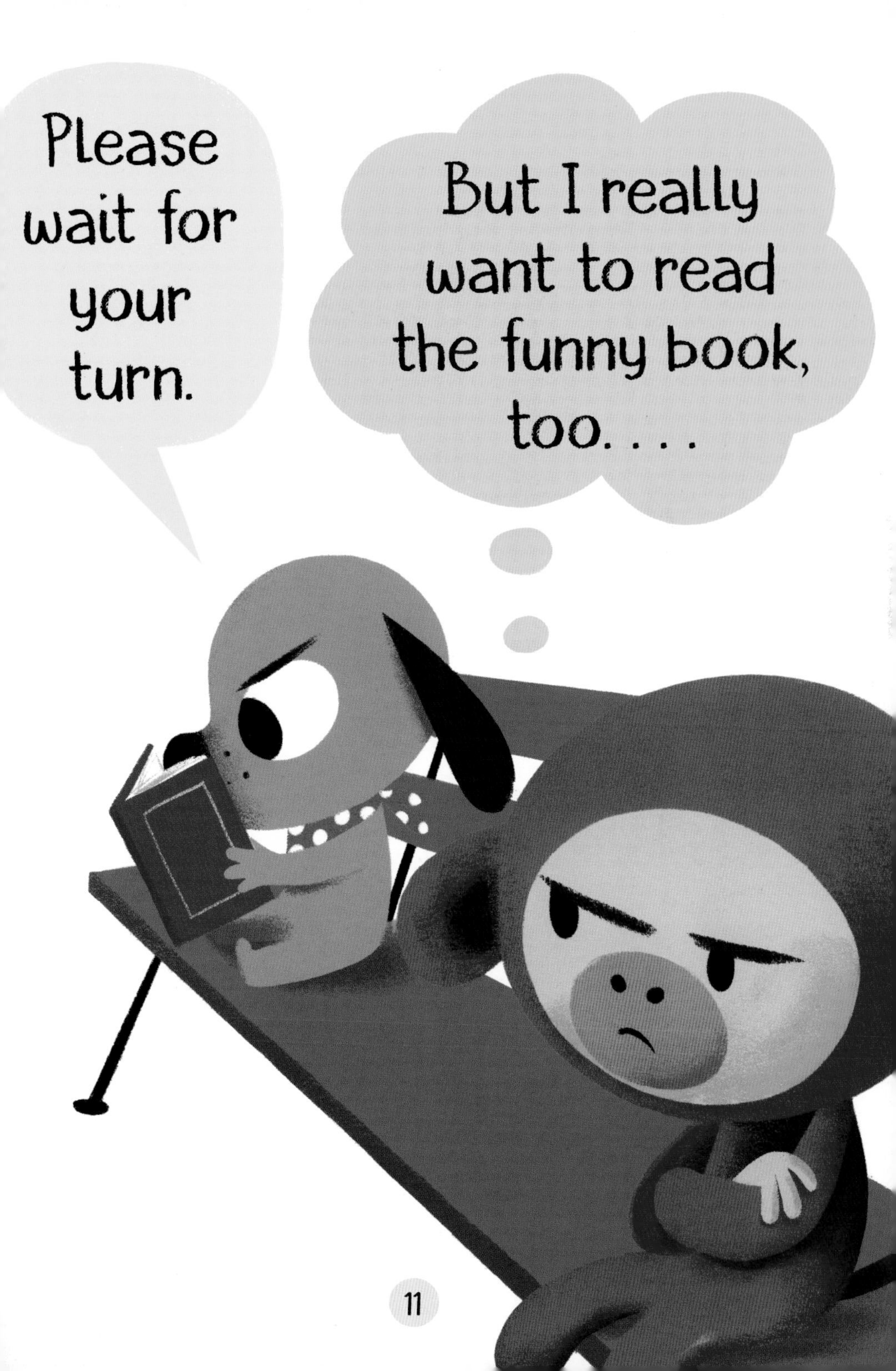
Please wait for your turn.
But I really want to read the funny book, too. . . .

Chapter 2
Not So Funny

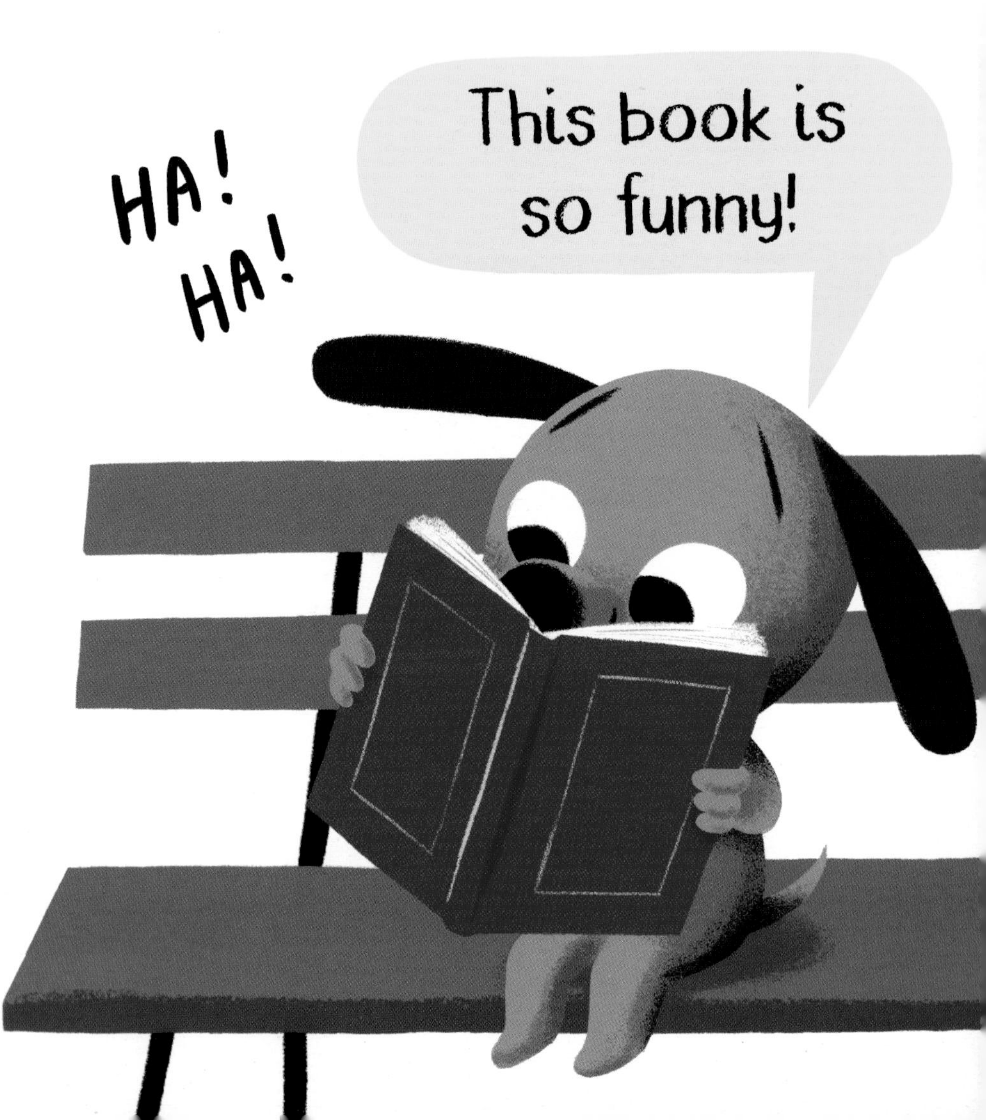
HA!
HA!
This book is so funny!

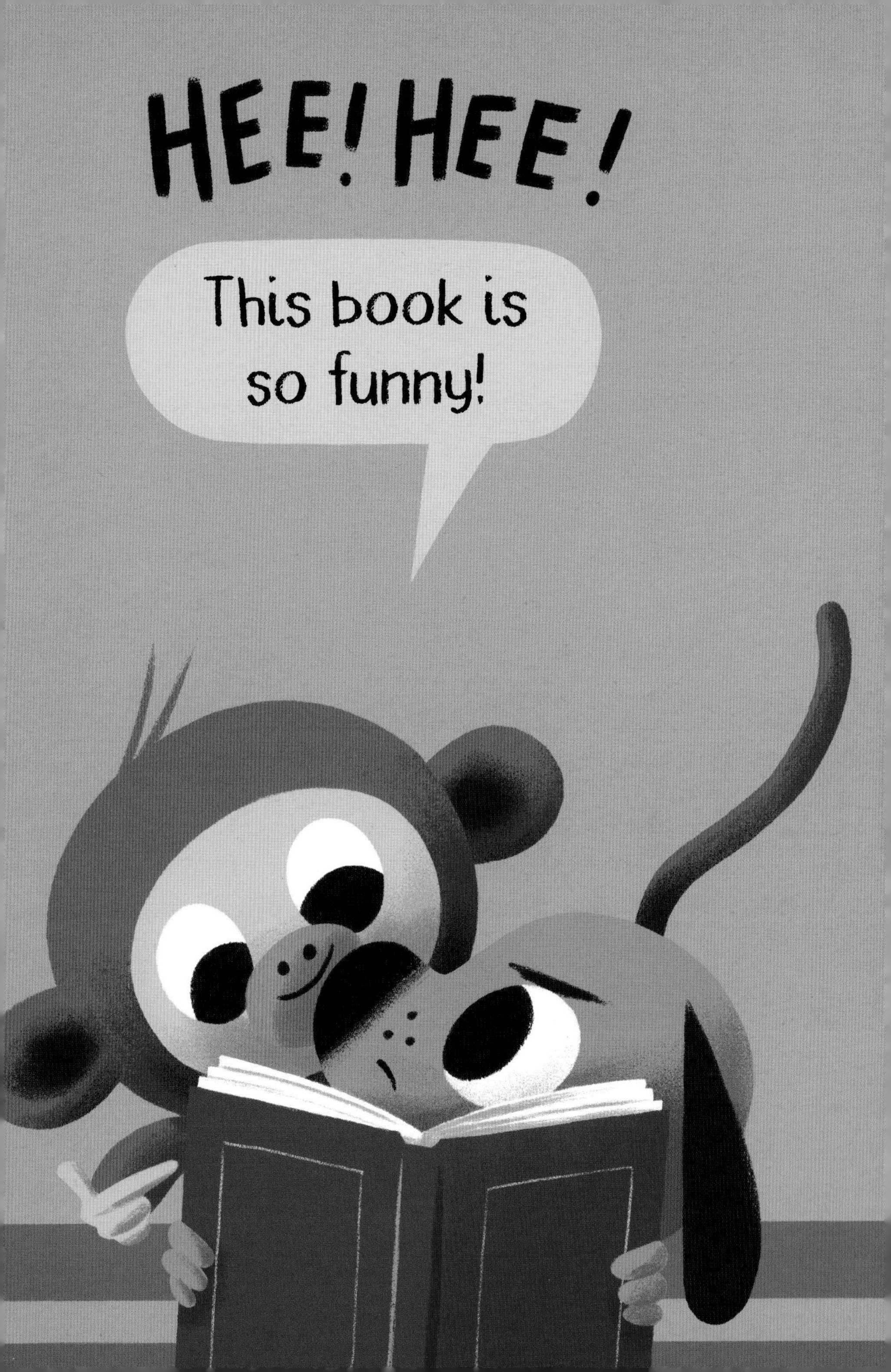
HEE! HEE!
This book is so funny!

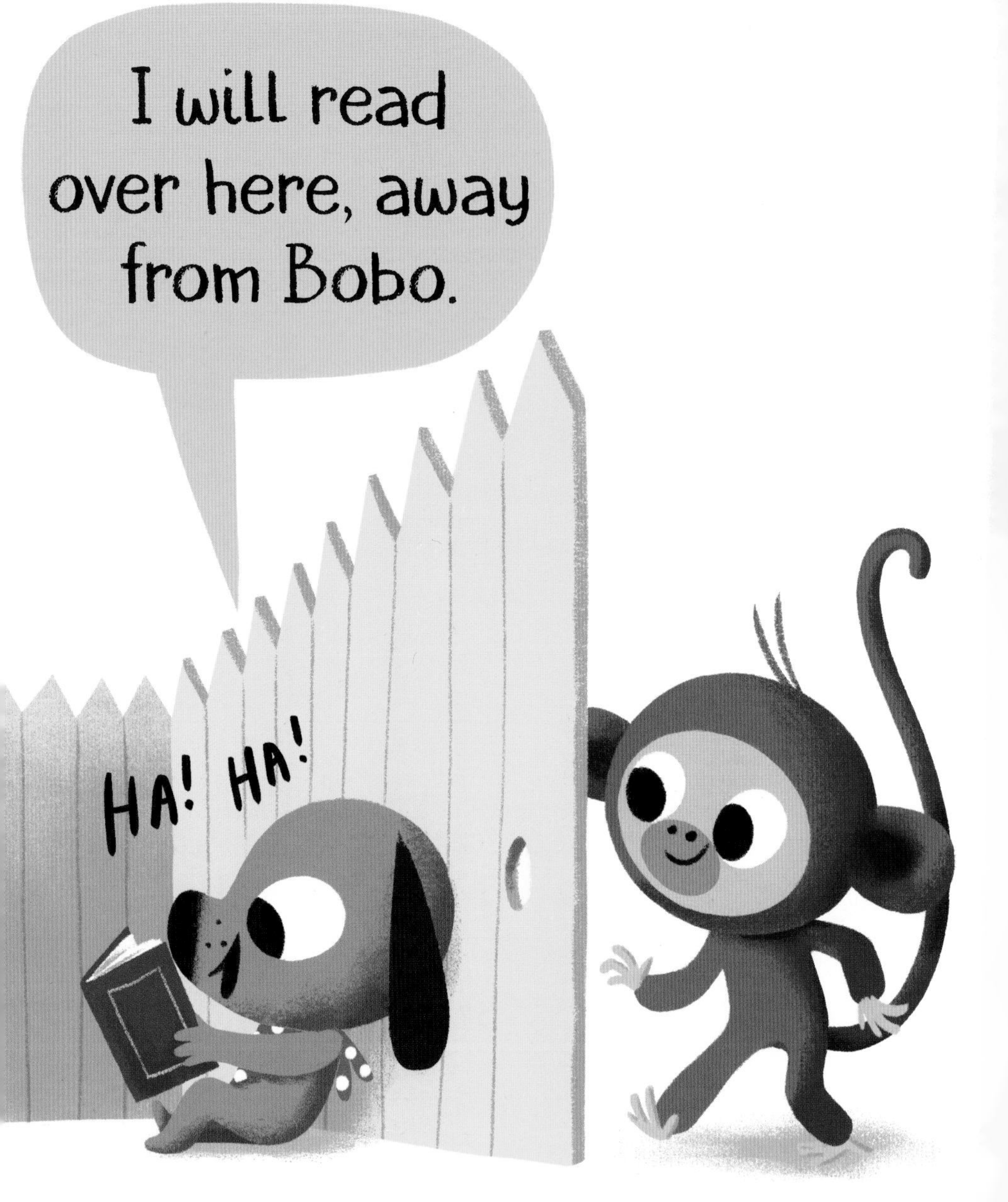
I will read over here, away from Bobo.
HA! HA!

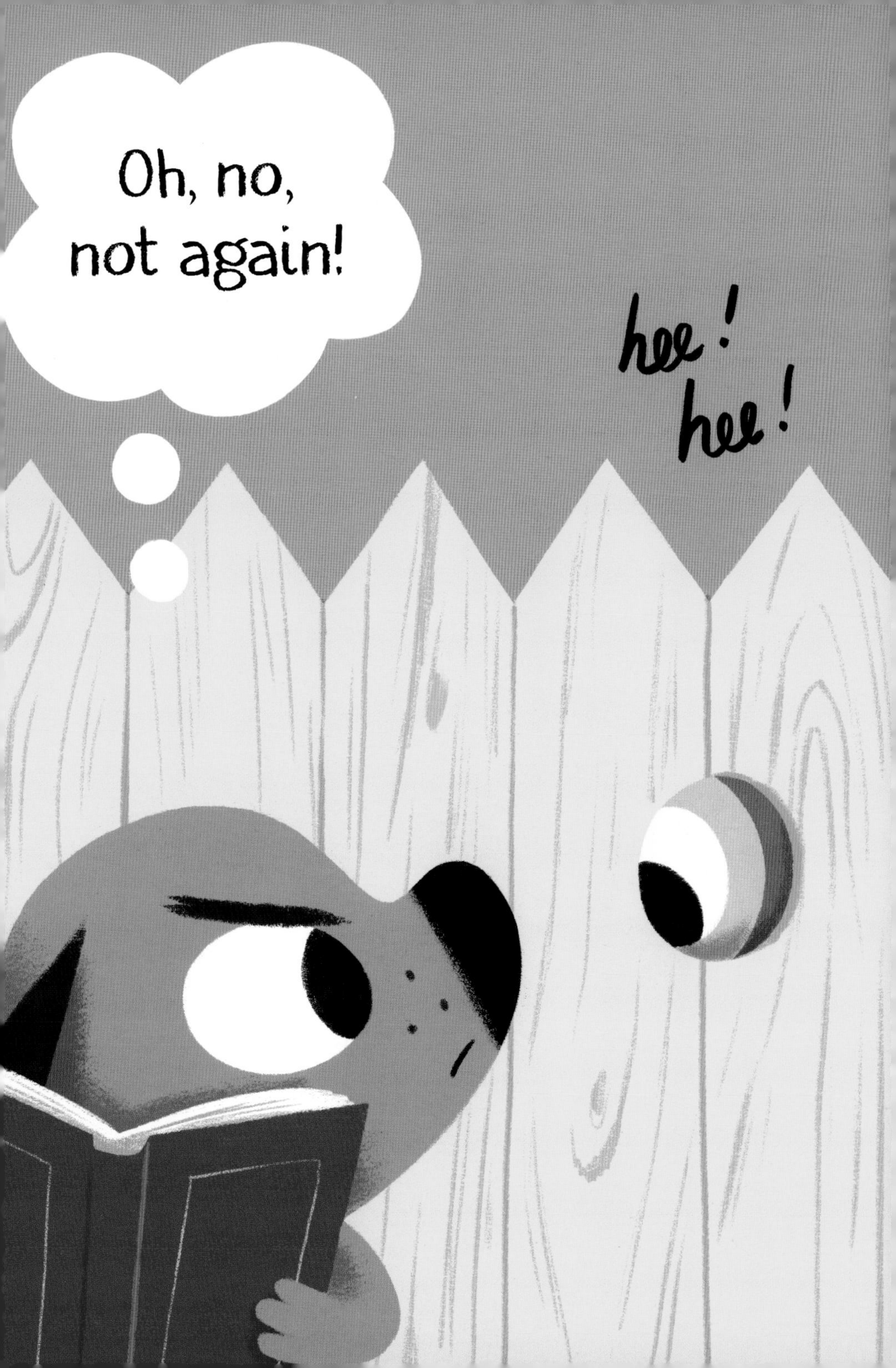
Oh, no,
not again!
hee!
hee!

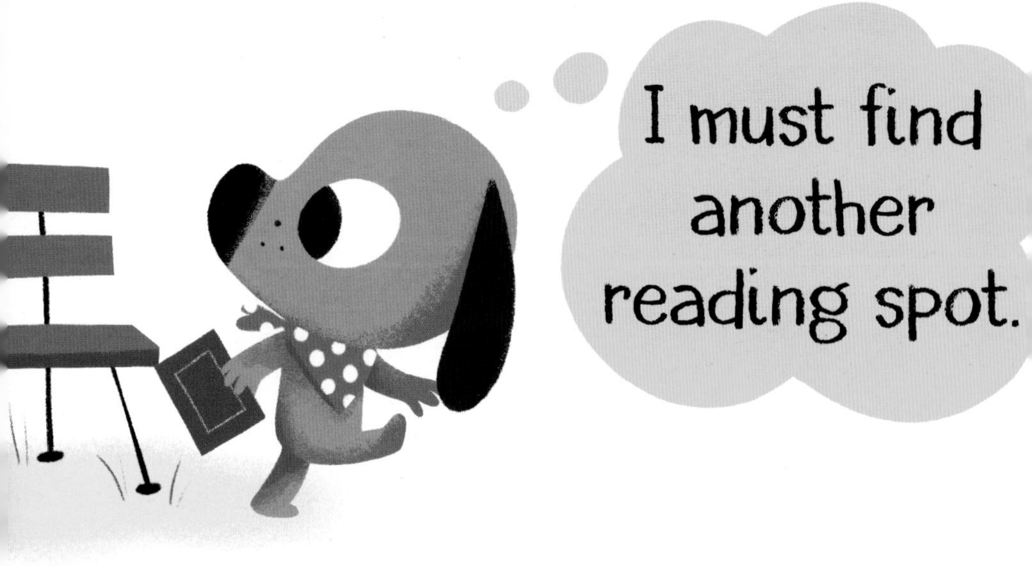
I must find another reading spot.

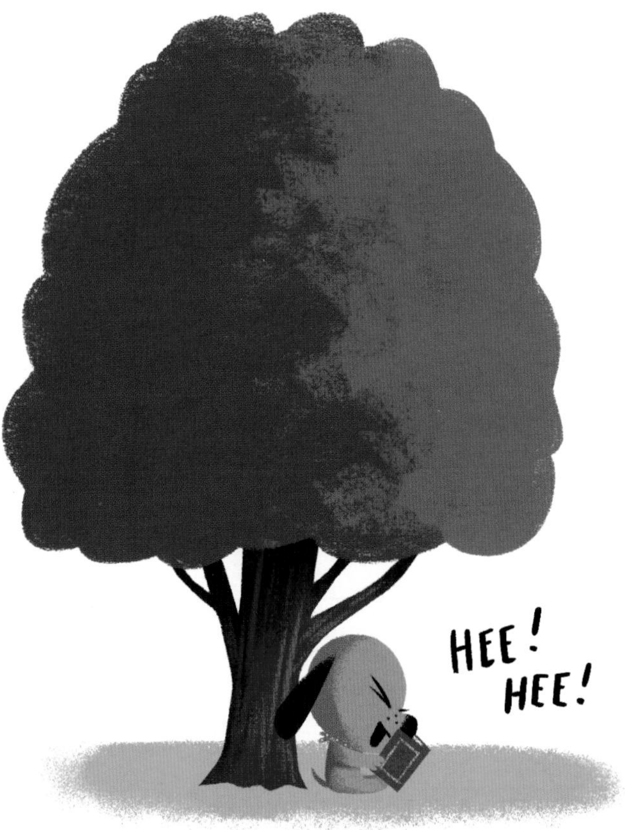
HEE! HEE!

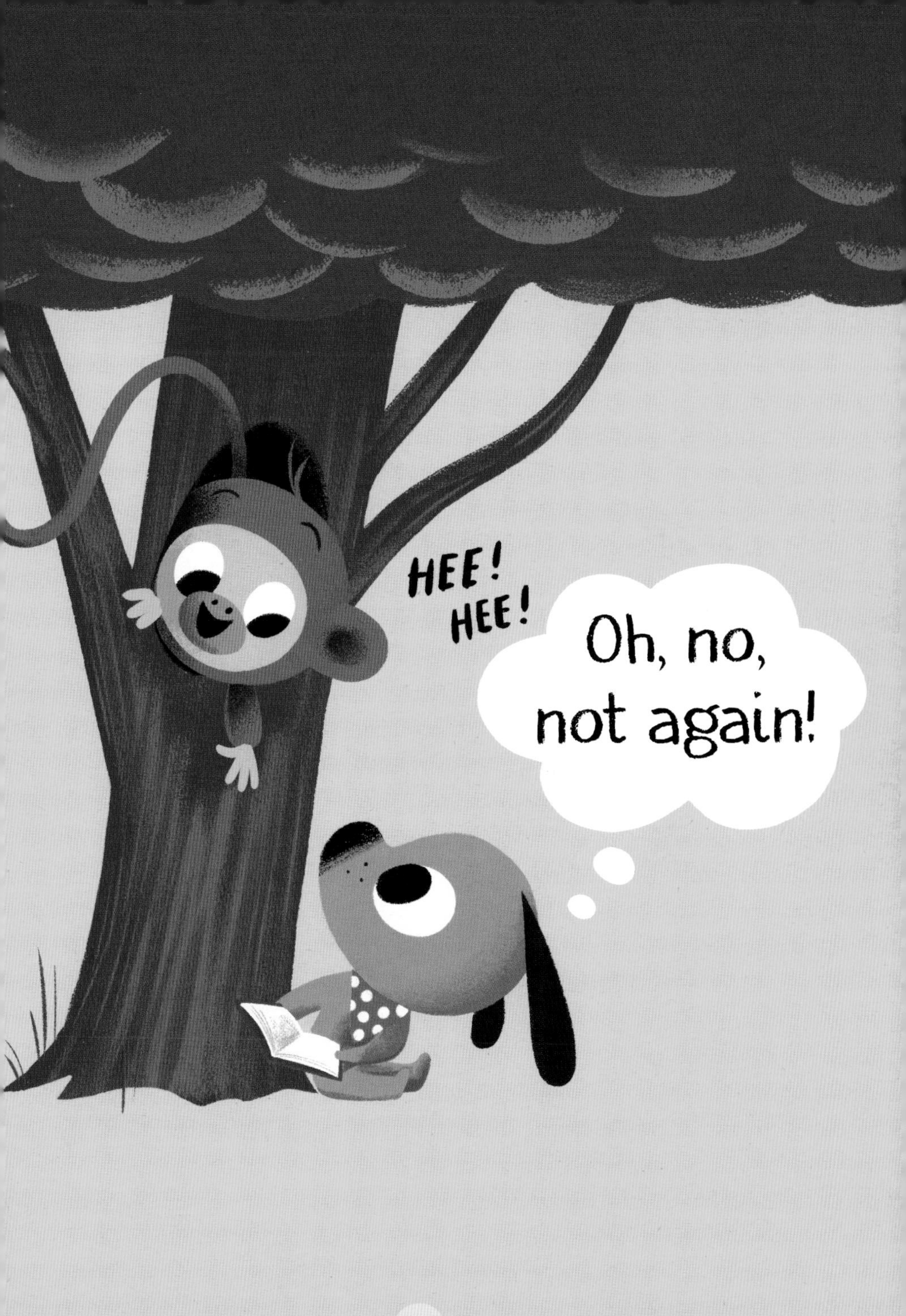
HEE!
HEE!
Oh, no,
not again!

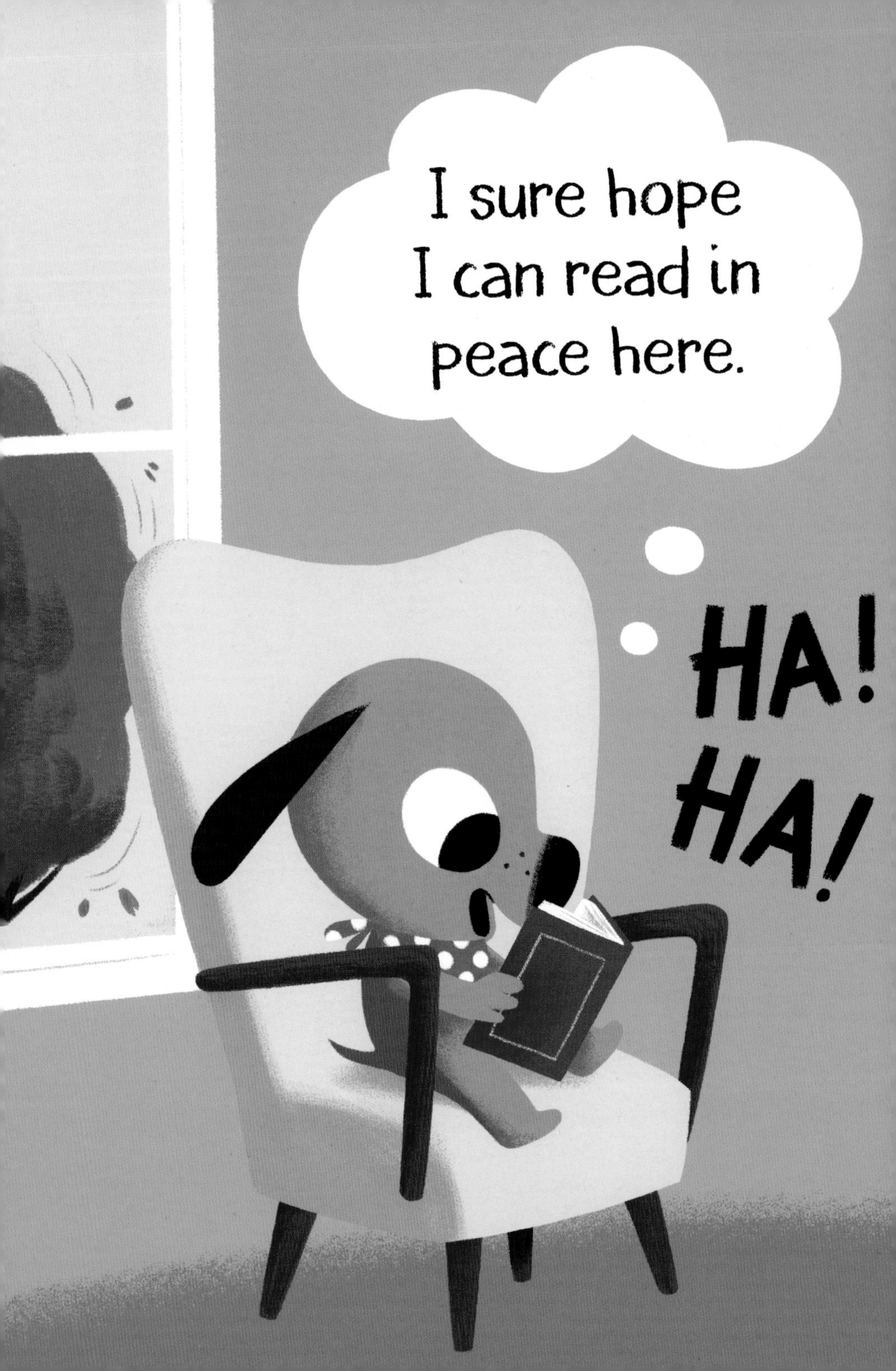
I sure hope I can read in peace here.
HA! HA!

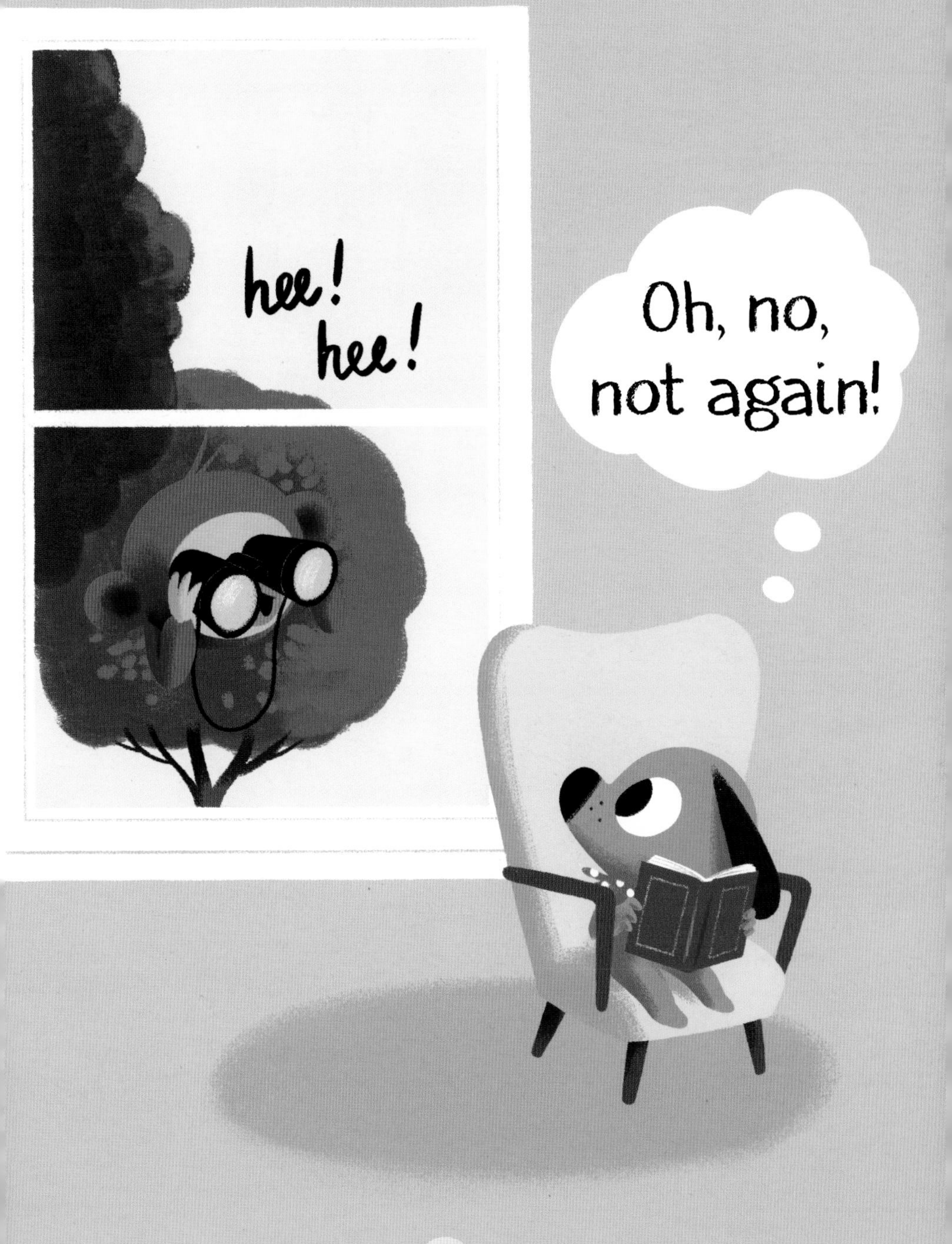
hee! hee!
Oh, no, not again!

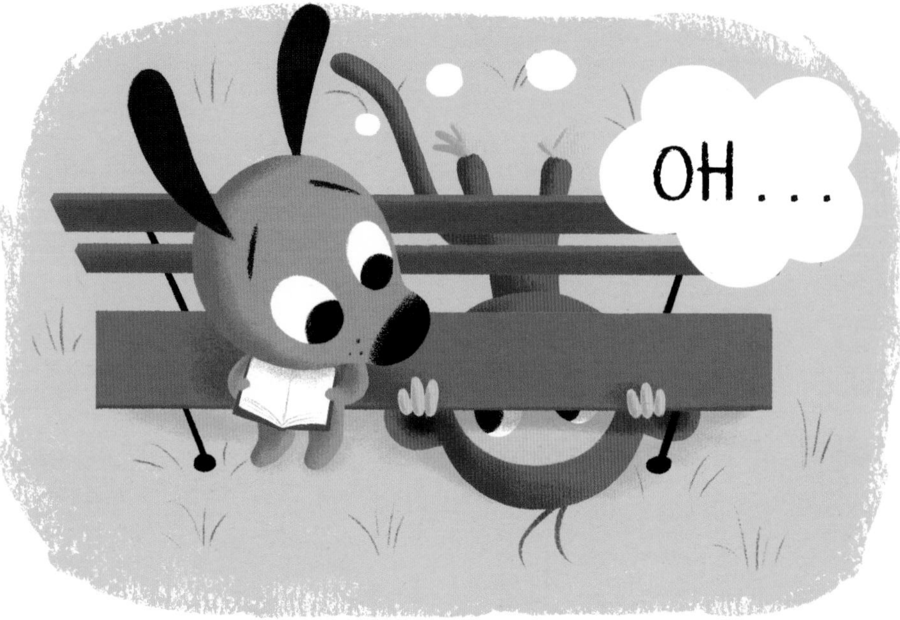
OH . . .

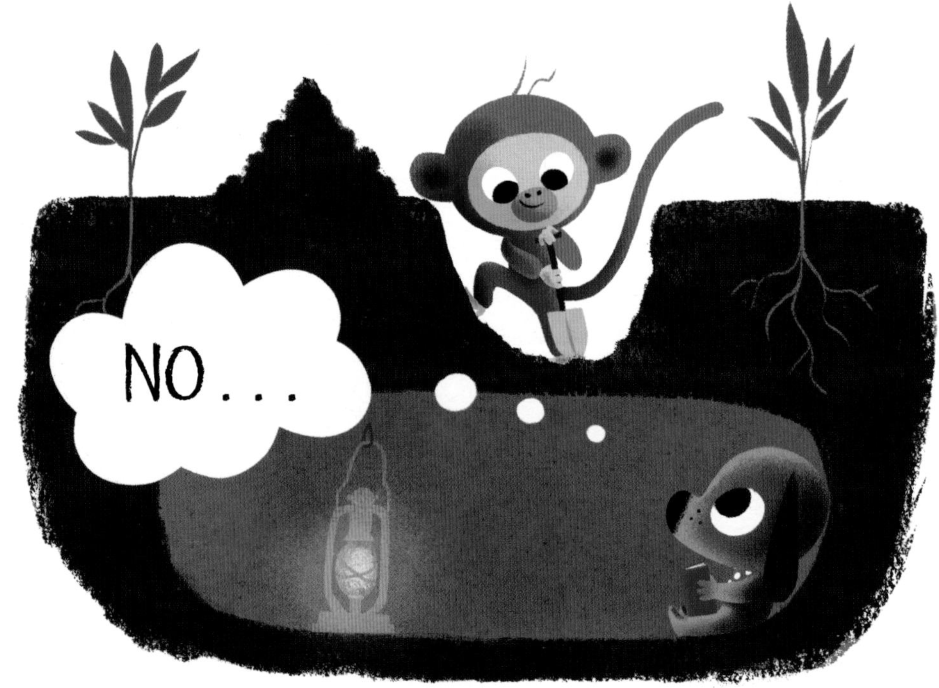
NO . . .

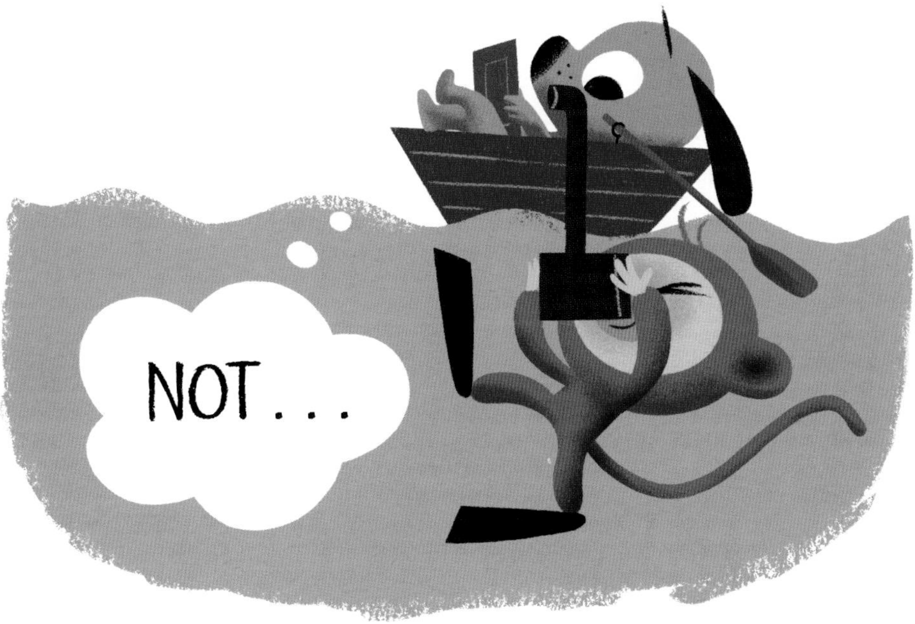
NOT . . .

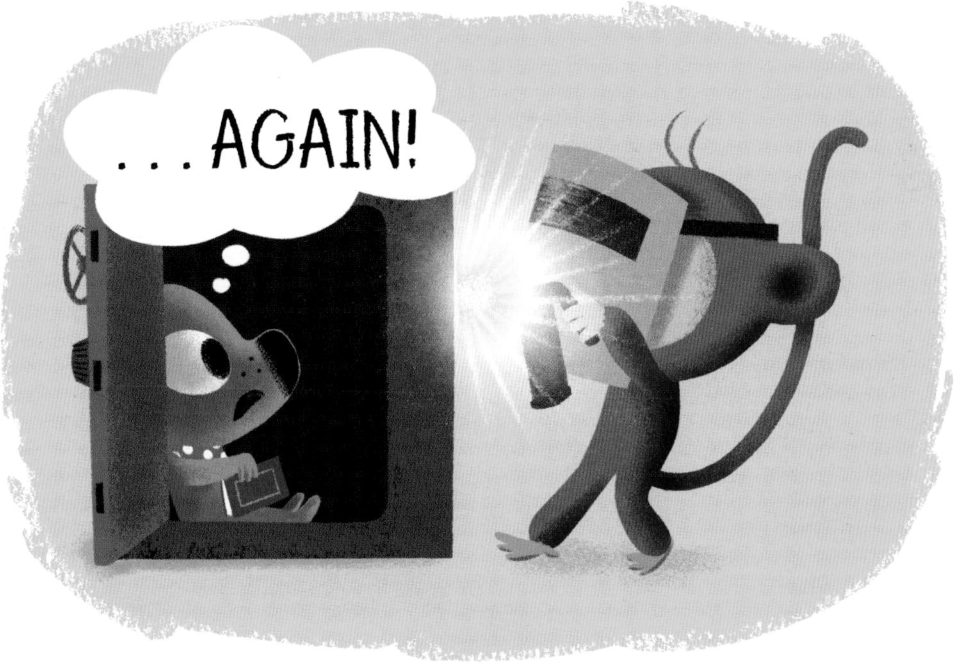
. . . AGAIN!

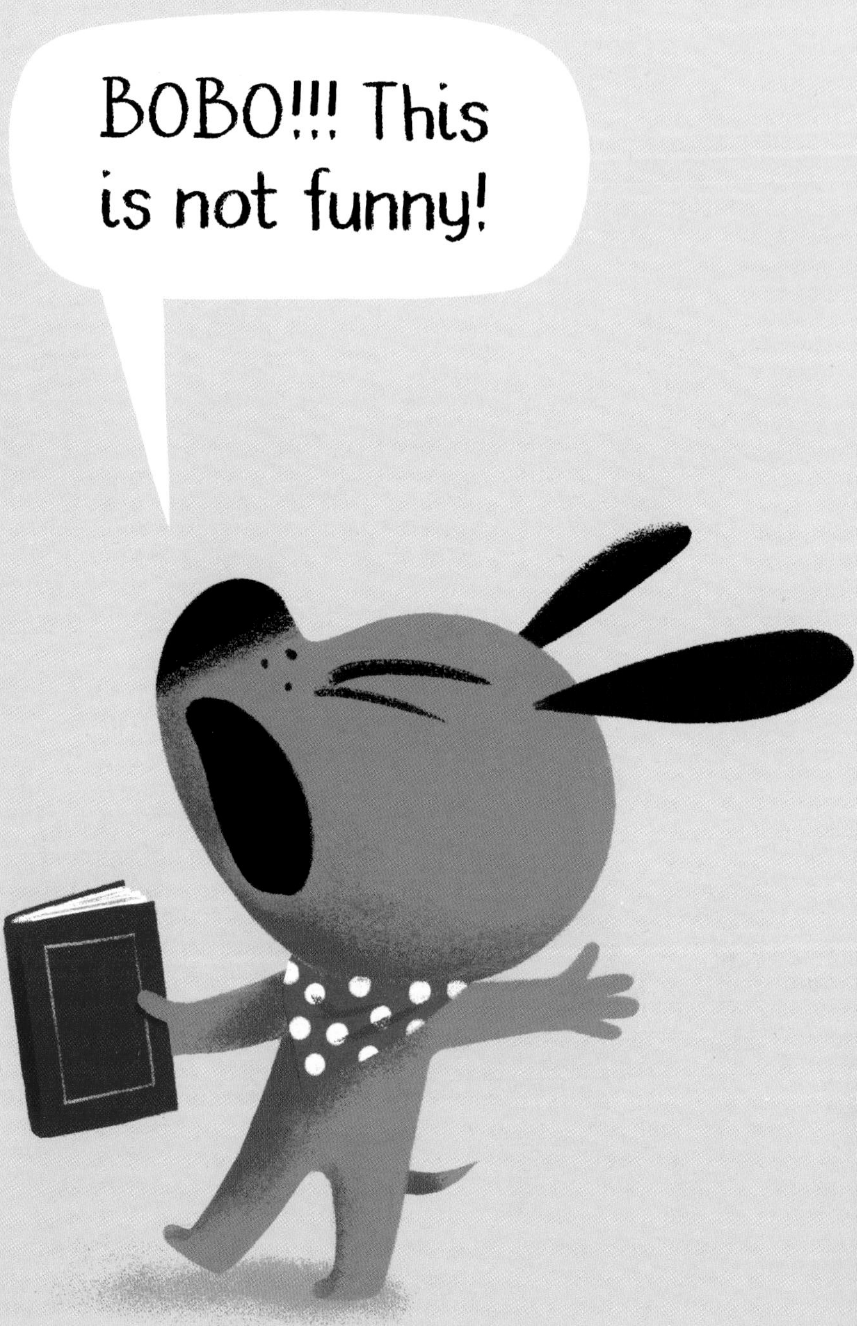
BOBO!!! This is not funny!

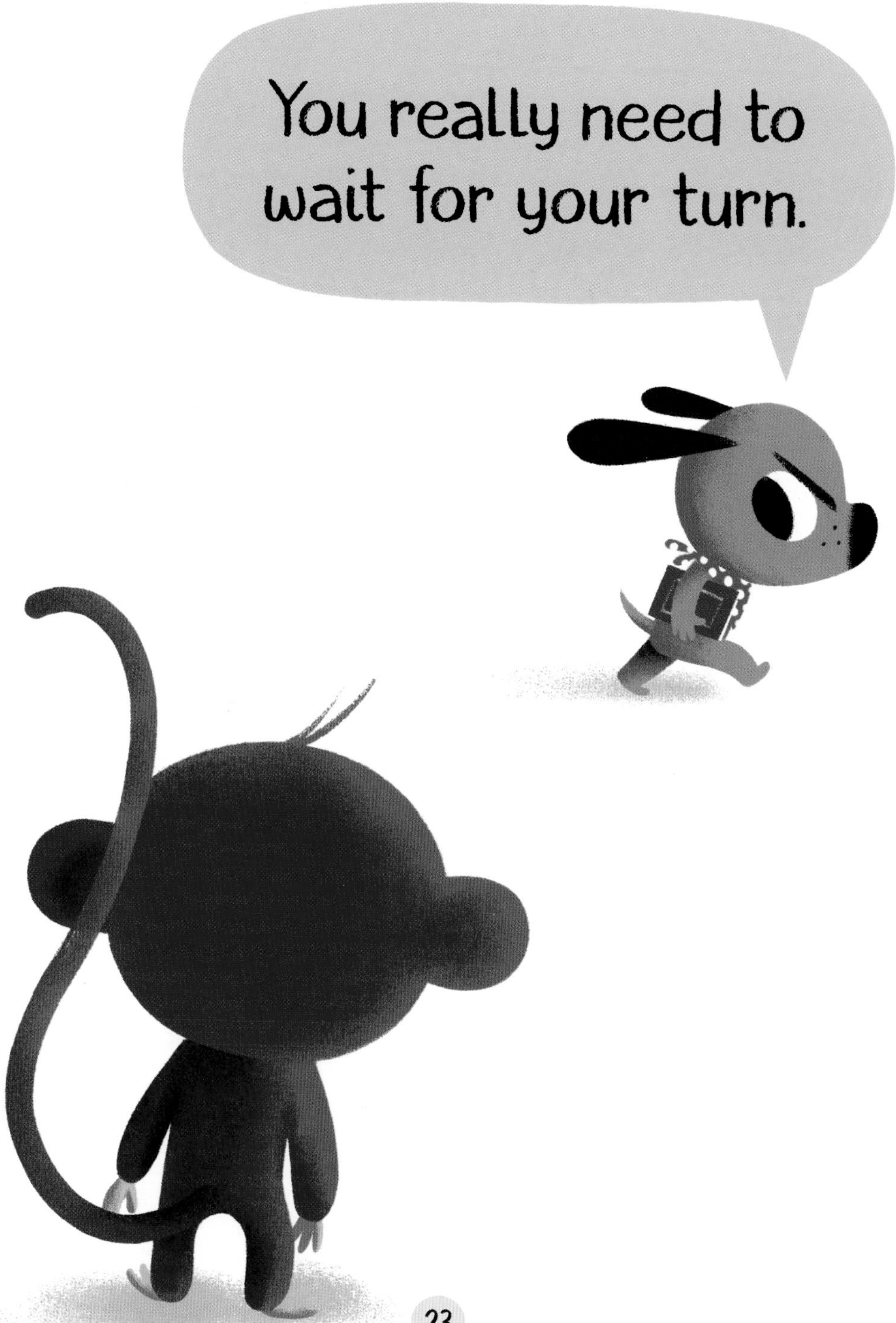
You really need to wait for your turn.

Chapter 3
Highly Funny

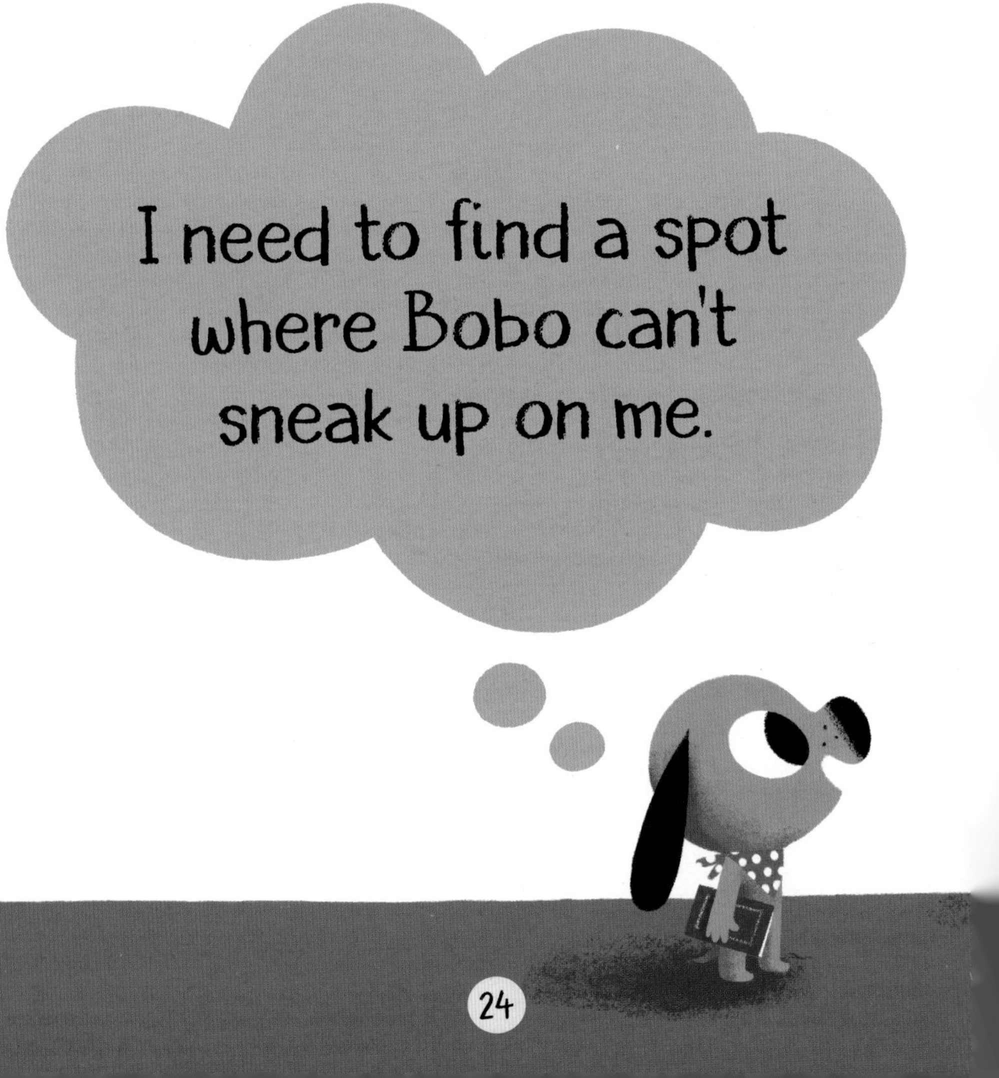
I need to find a spot where Bobo can't sneak up on me.

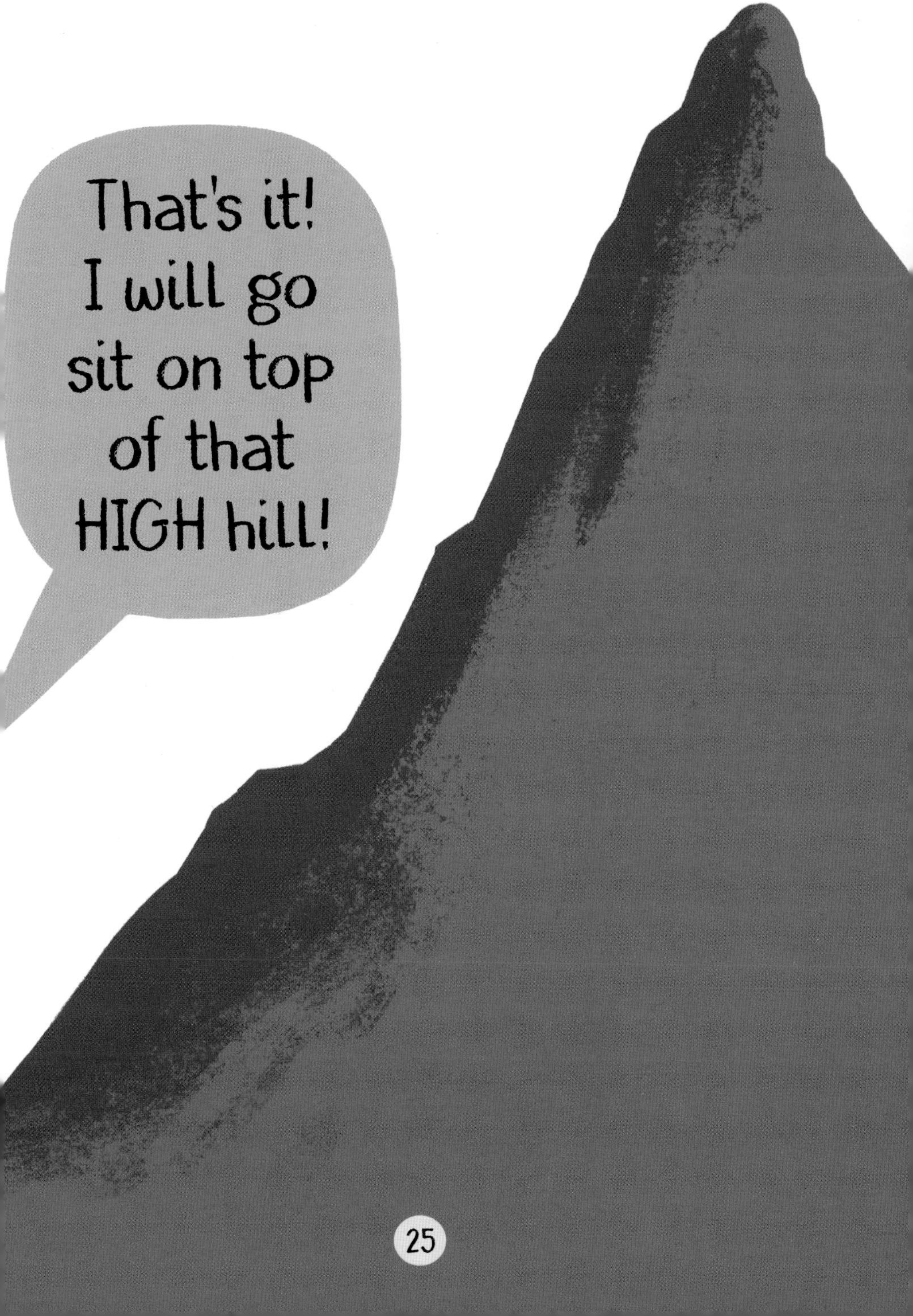
That's it! I will go sit on top of that HIGH hill!

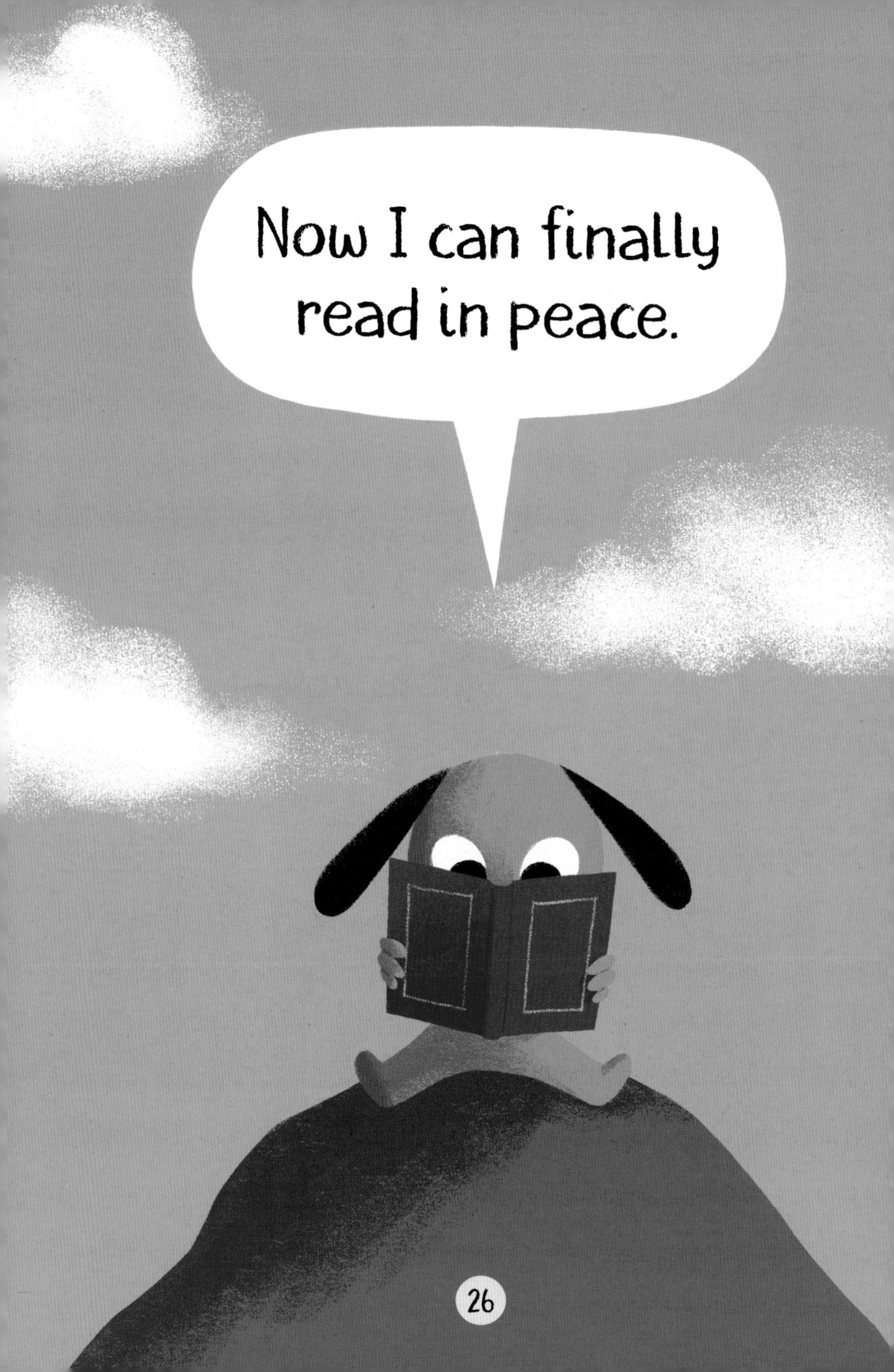
Now I can finally read in peace.

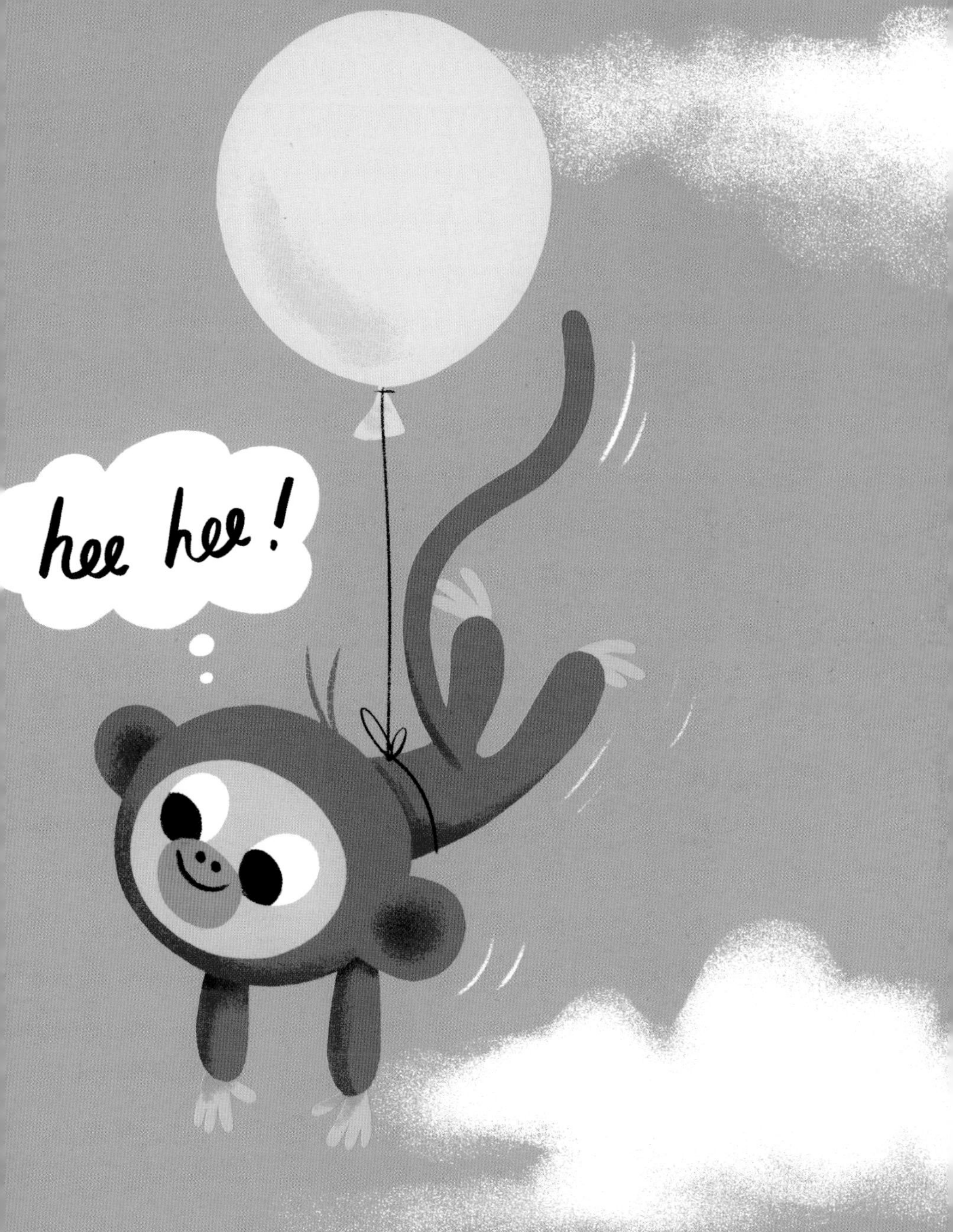
hee hee!

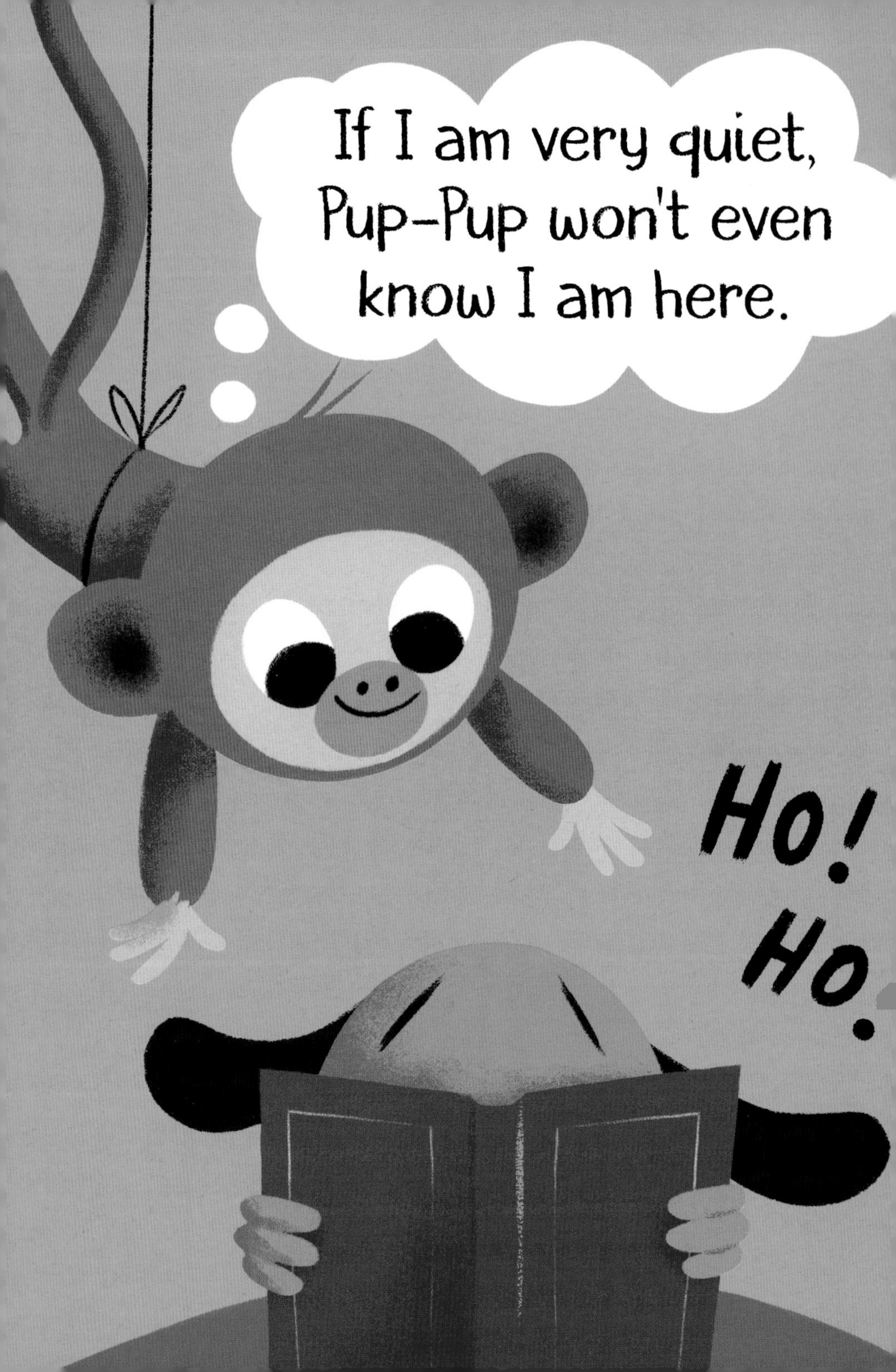
If I am very quiet, Pup-Pup won't even know I am here.
Ho! Ho.

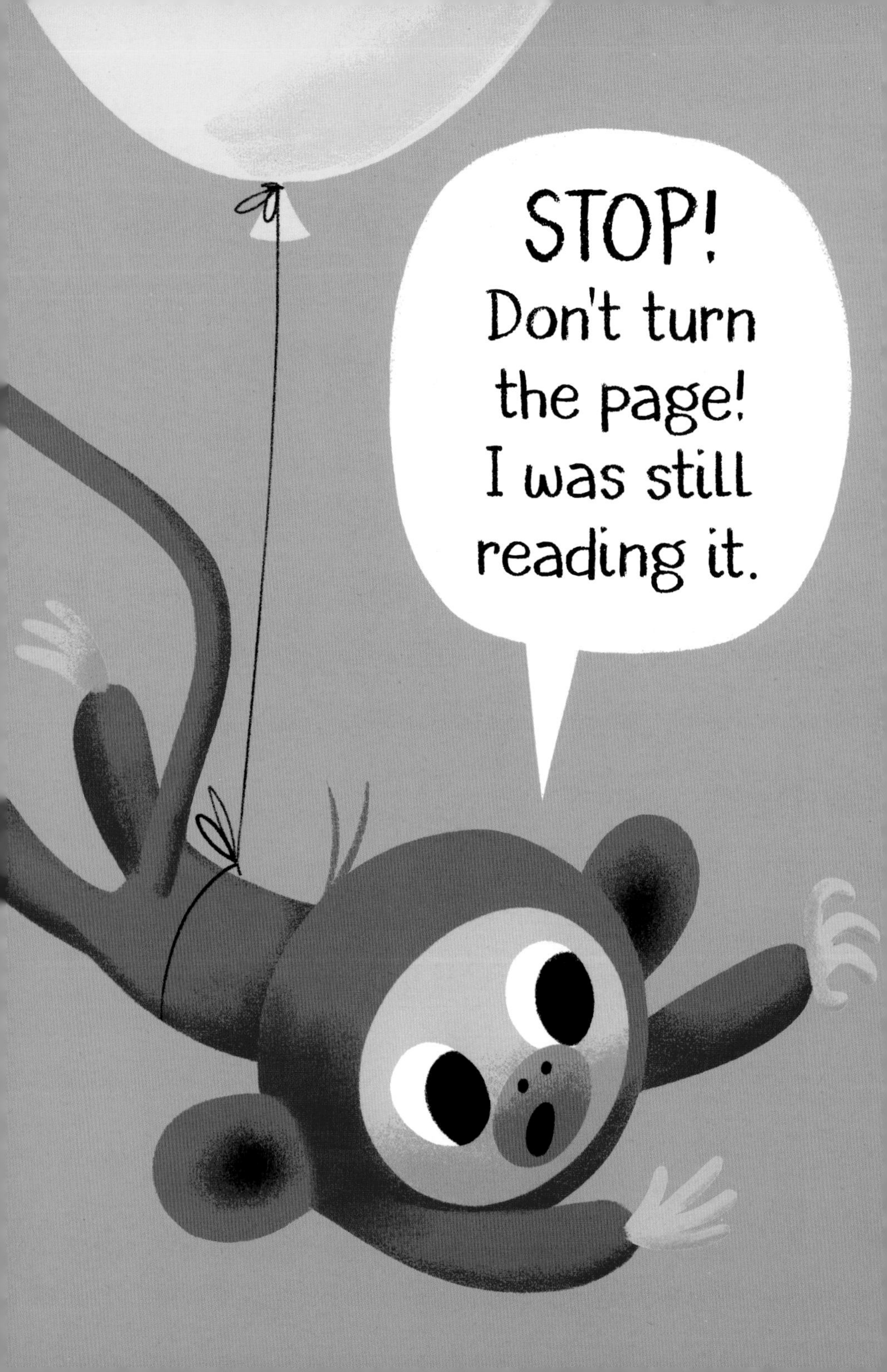
STOP!
Don't turn the page! I was still reading it.

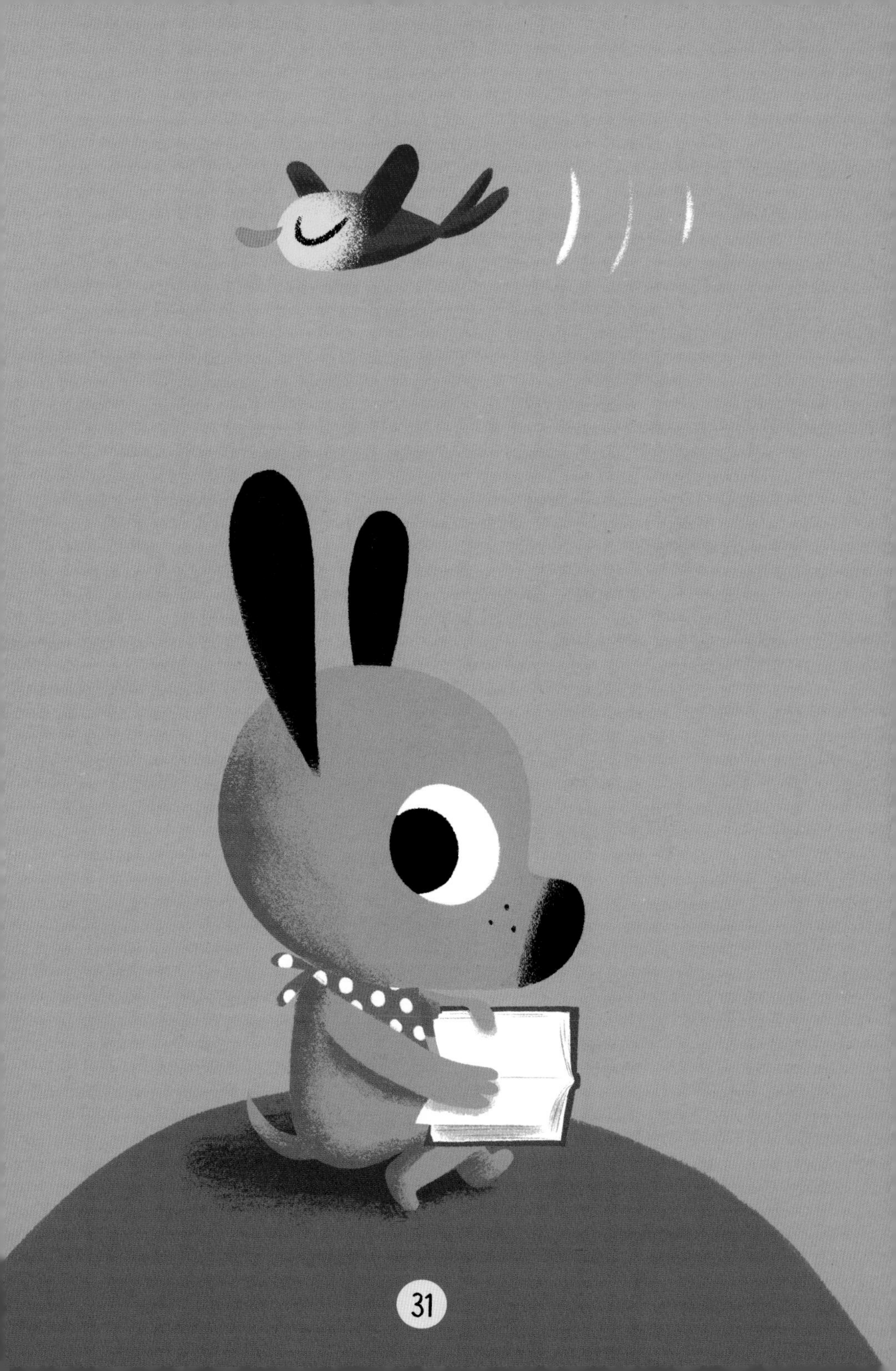

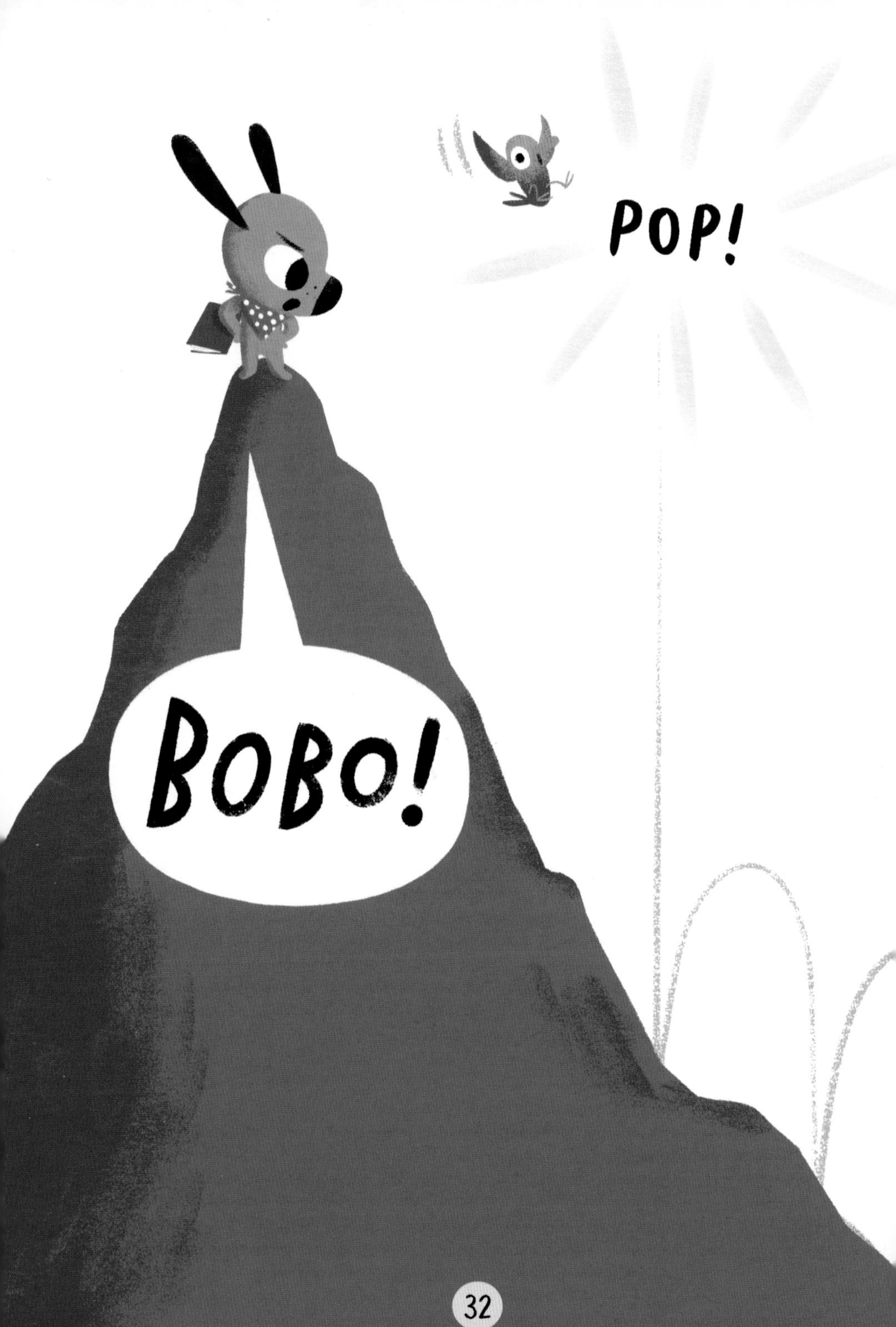
POP!
BOBO!

Chapter 4
My Funny Book

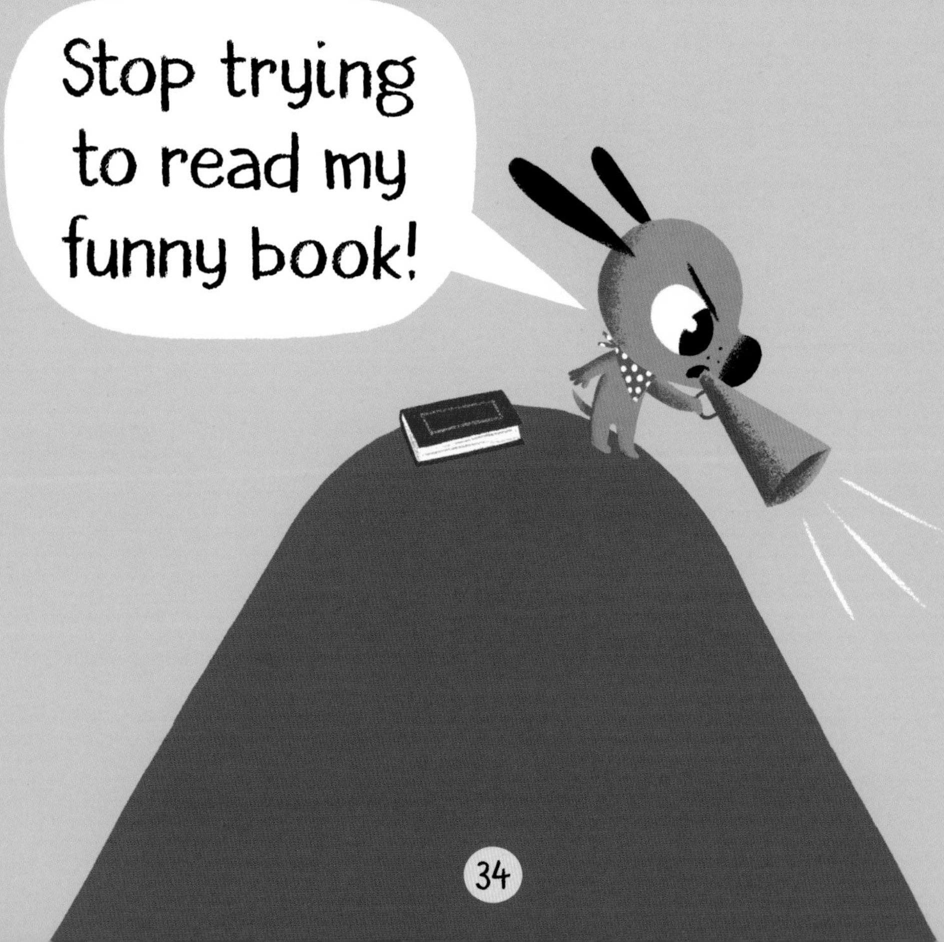
Stop trying to read my funny book!

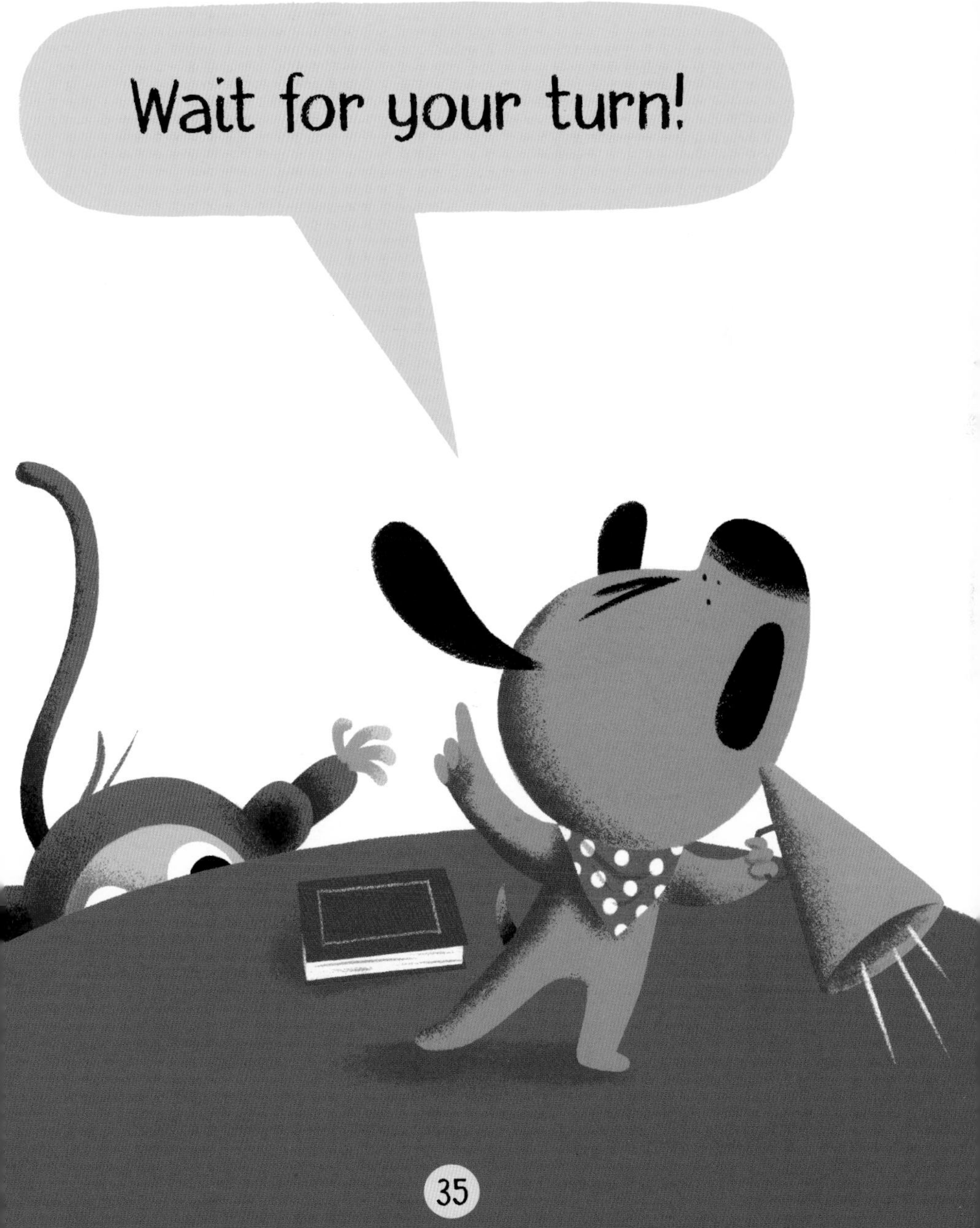
Wait for your turn!

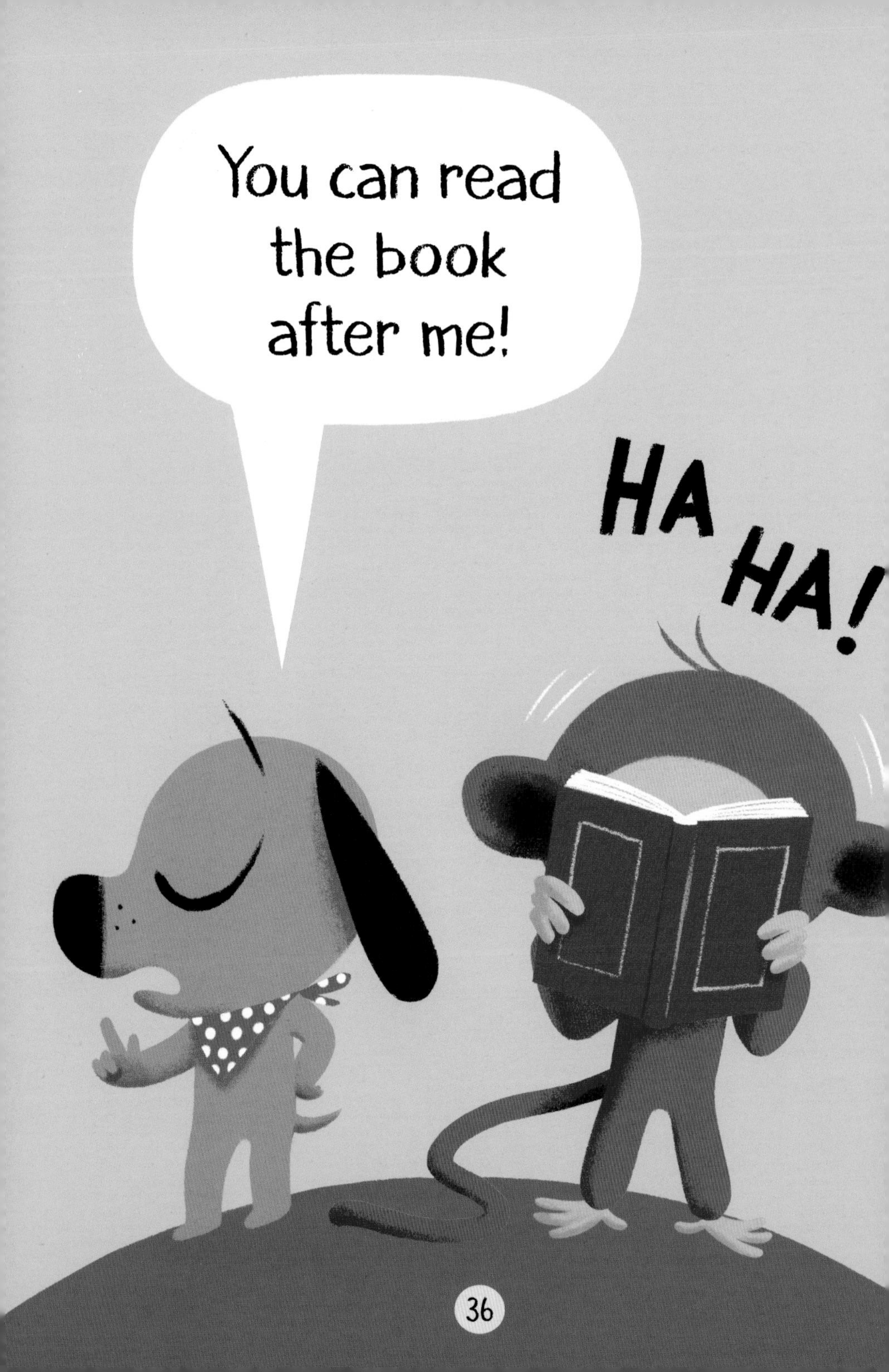
You can read the book after me!
HA HA!

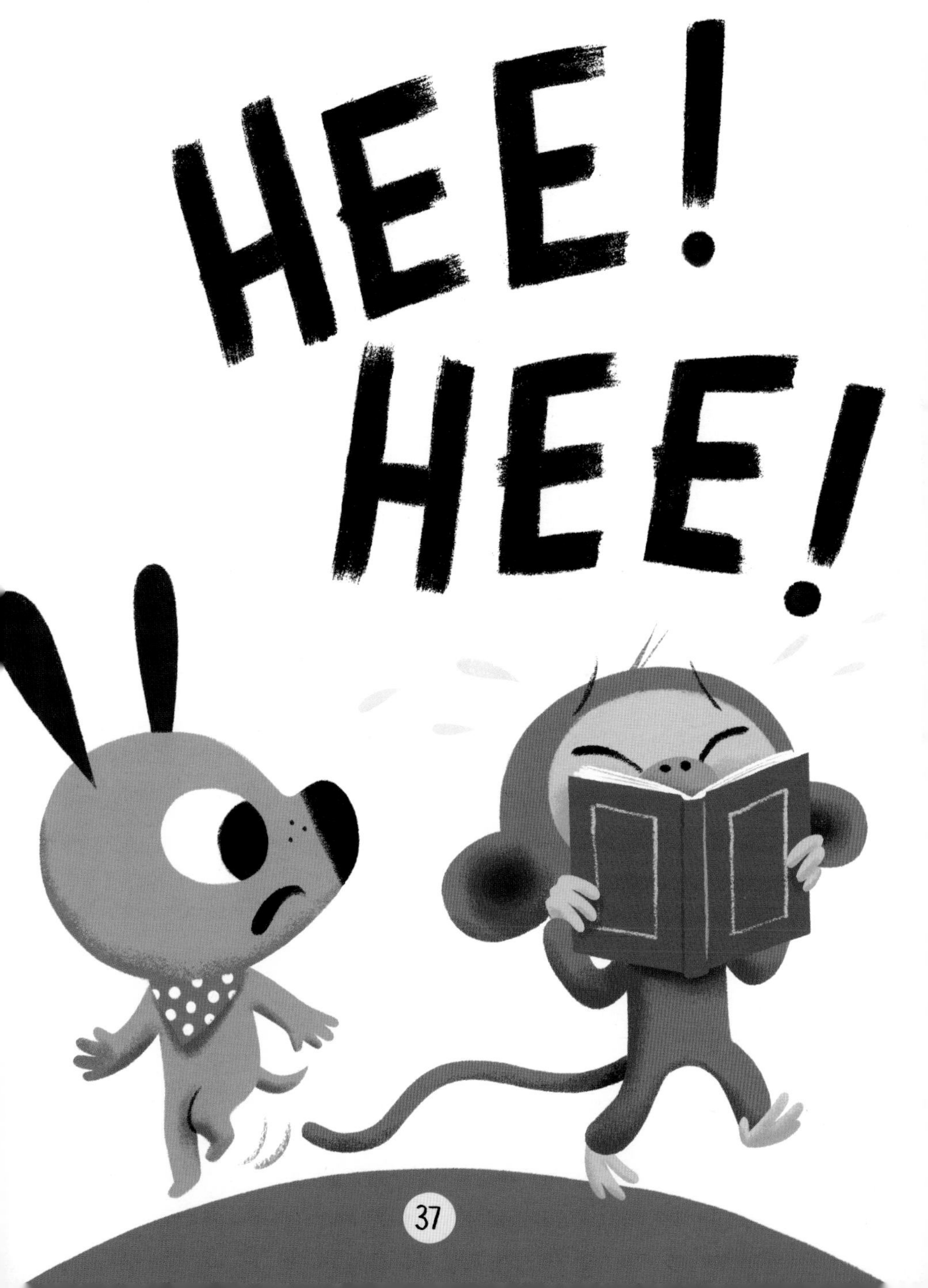
HEE!
HEE!

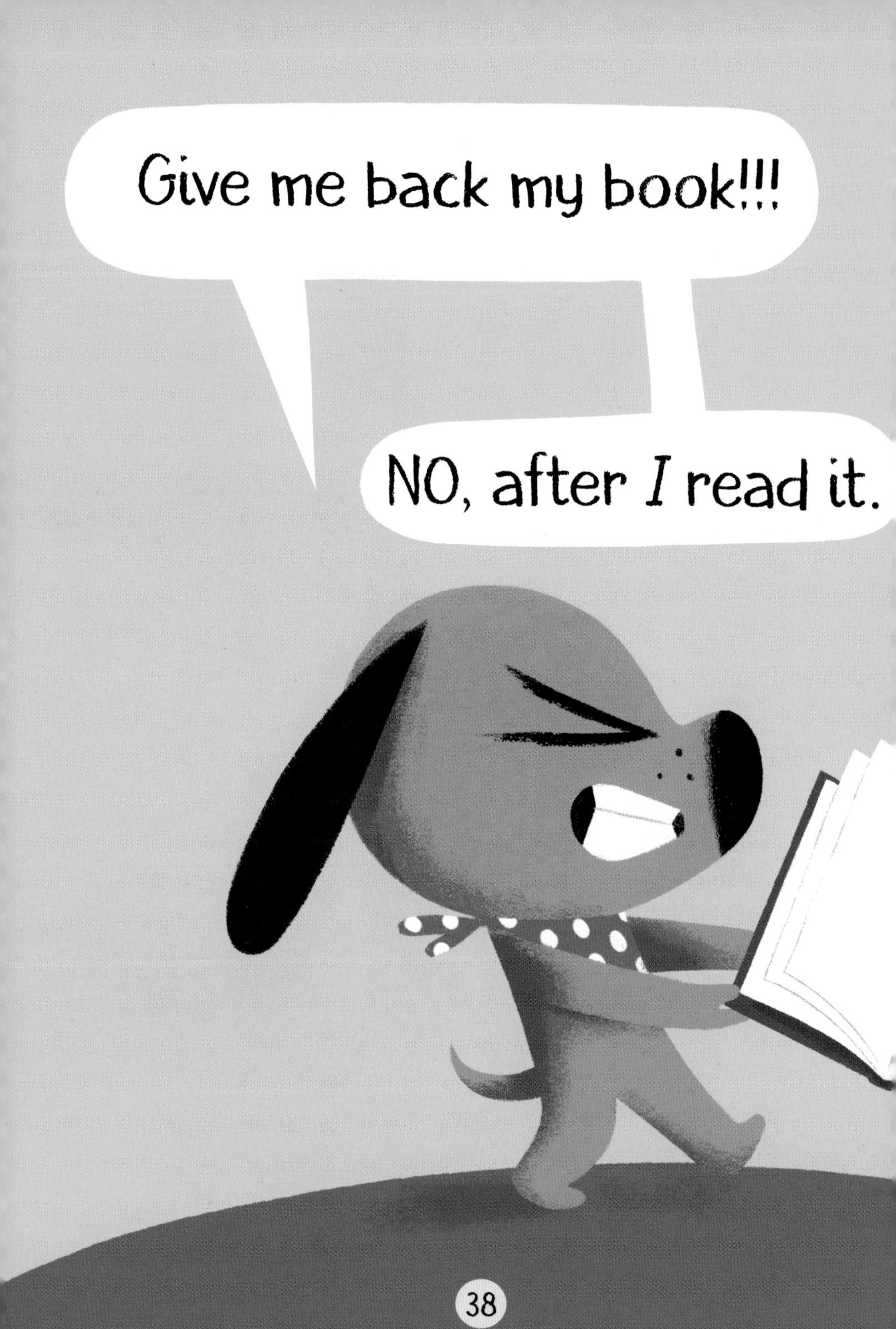
Give me back my book!!!
NO, after *I* read it.

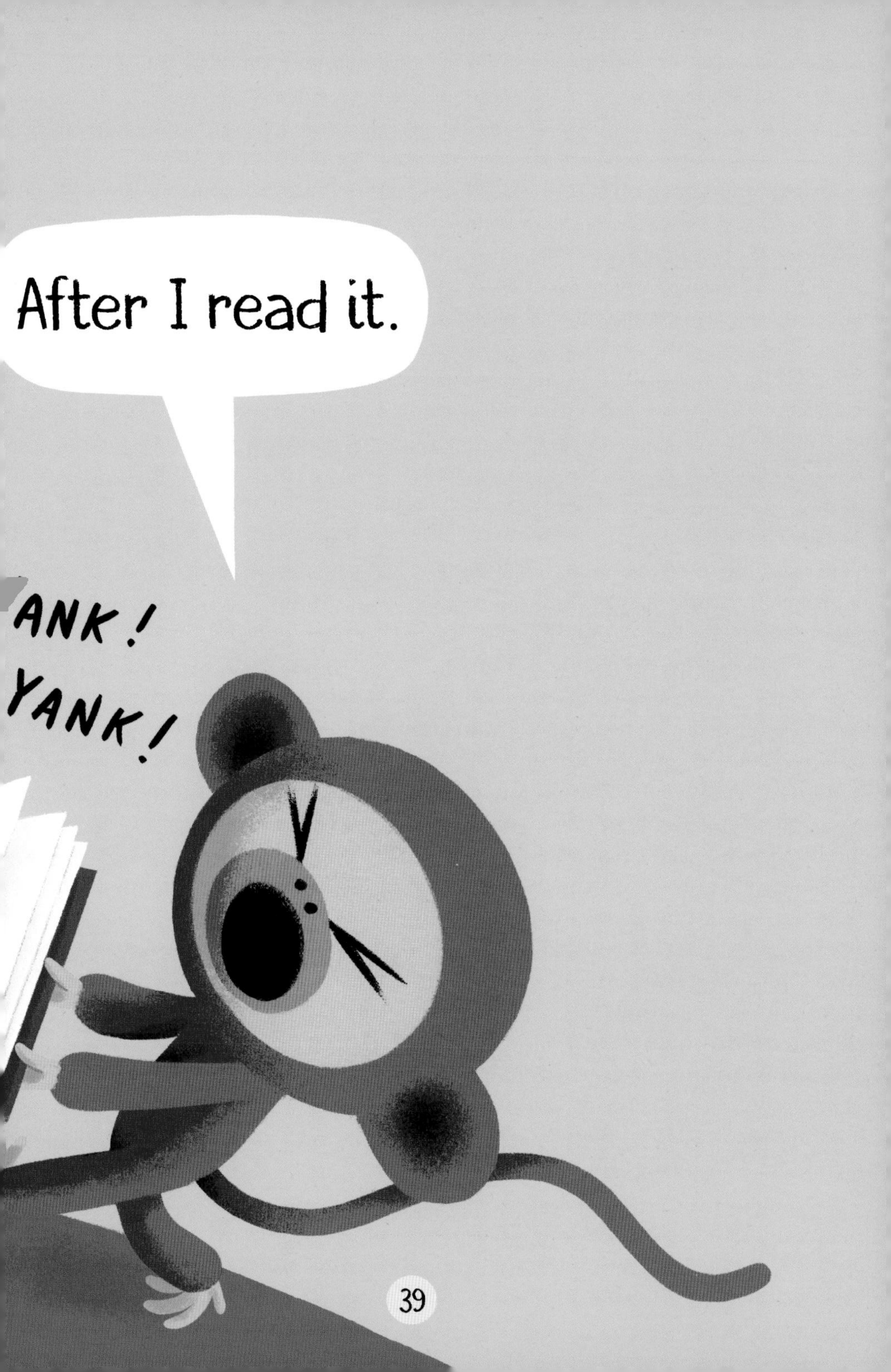
After I read it.
ANK!
YANK!

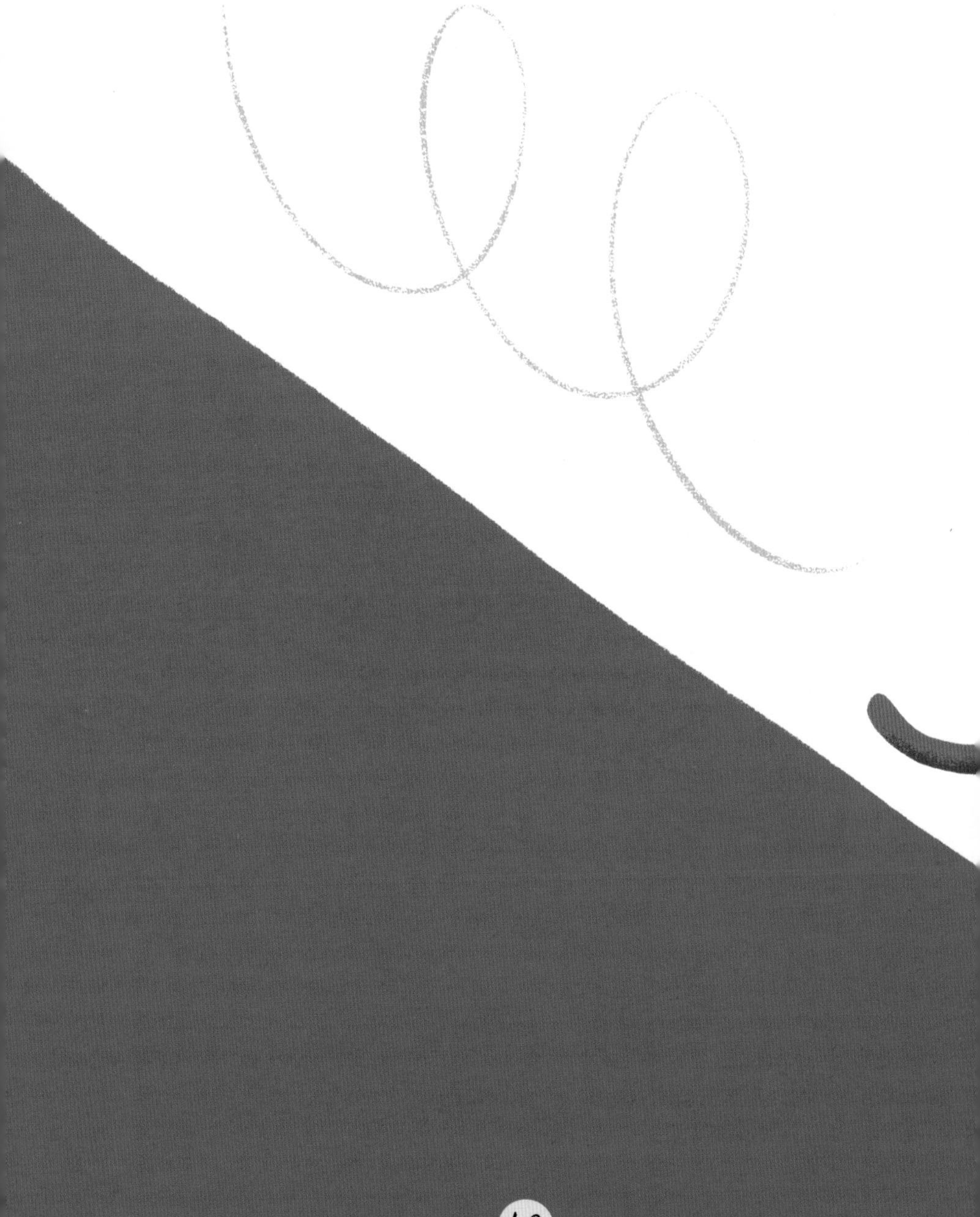

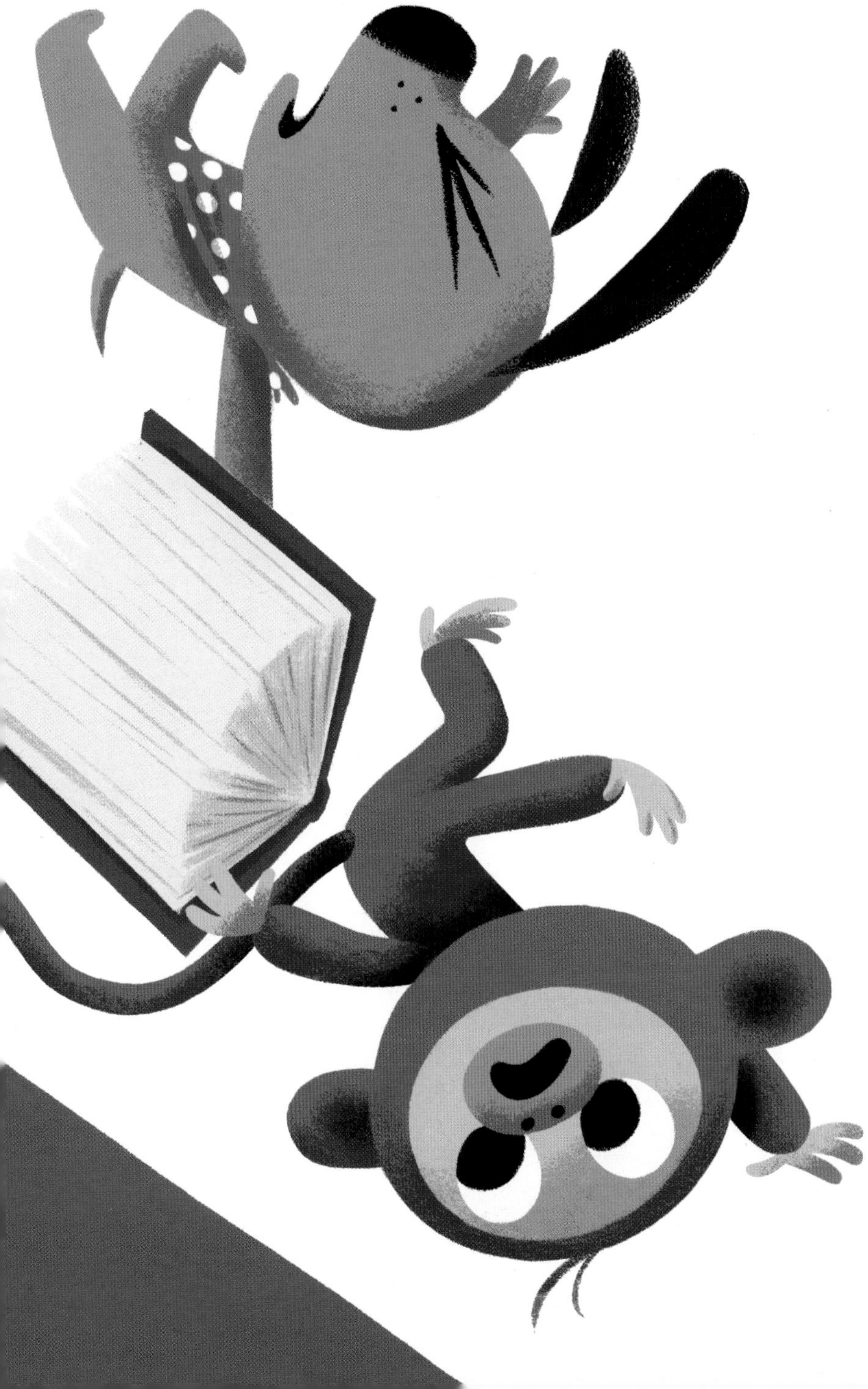

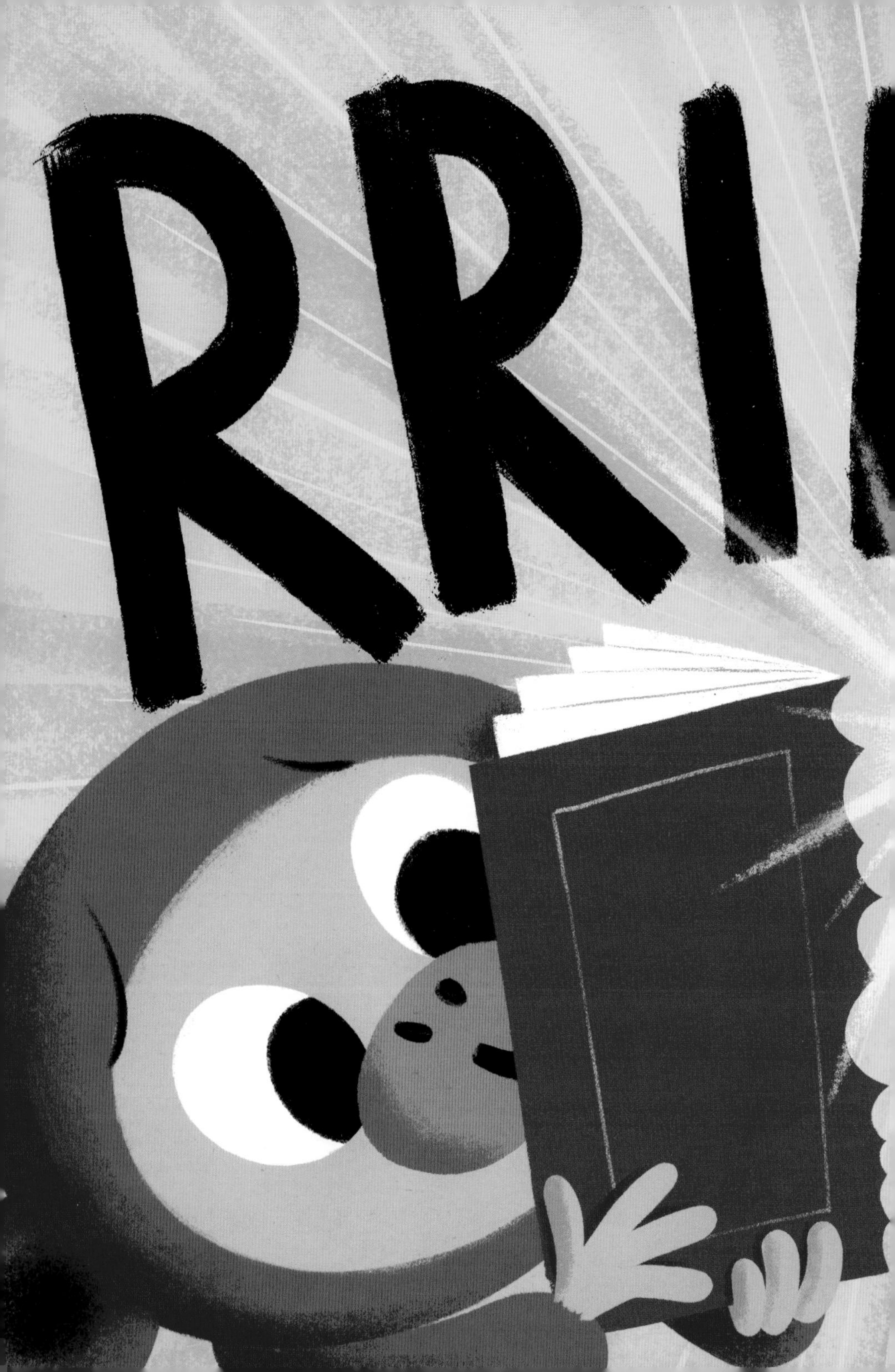
RRI

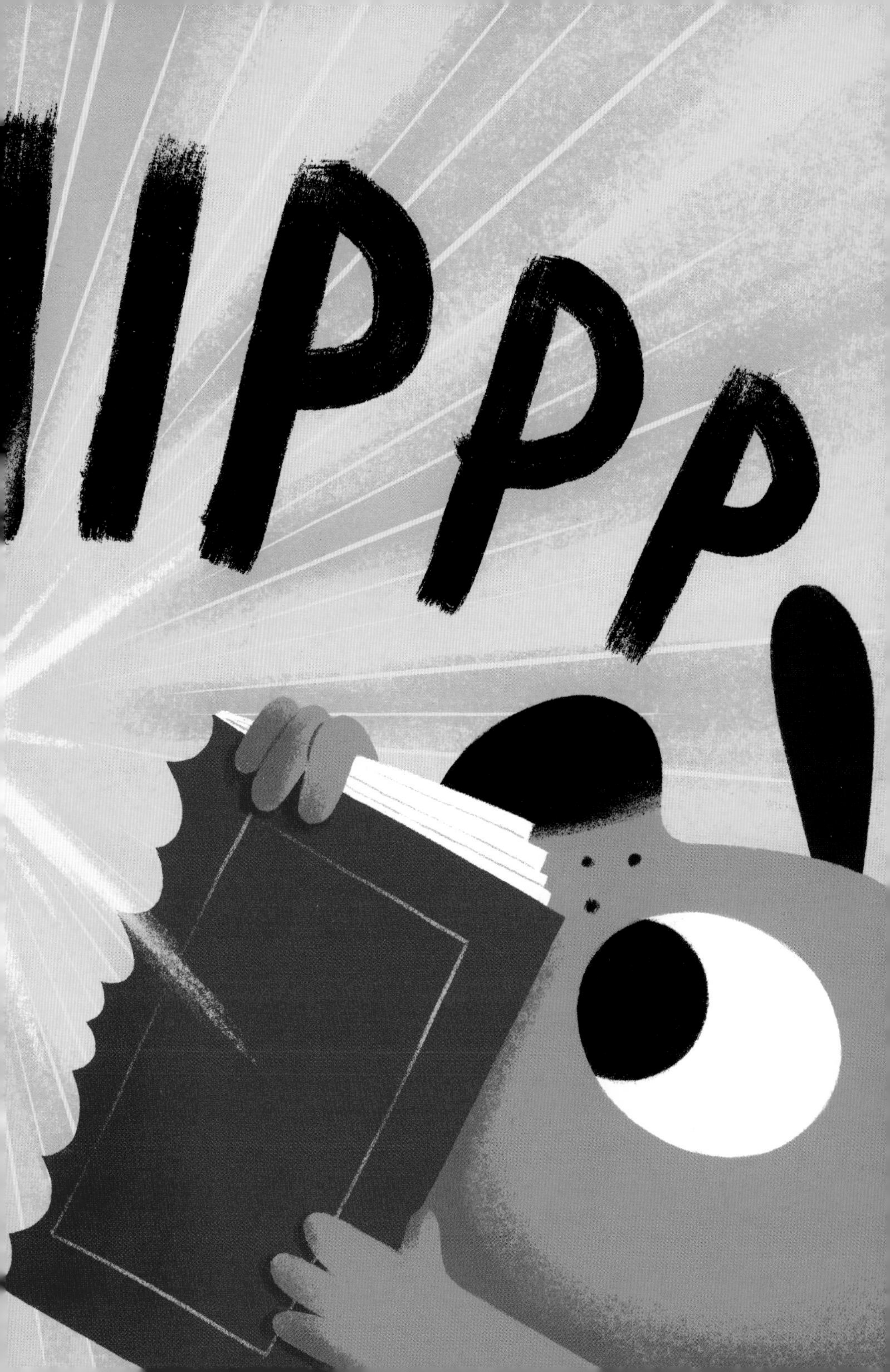
IIPPP

Chapter 5
Half as Funny

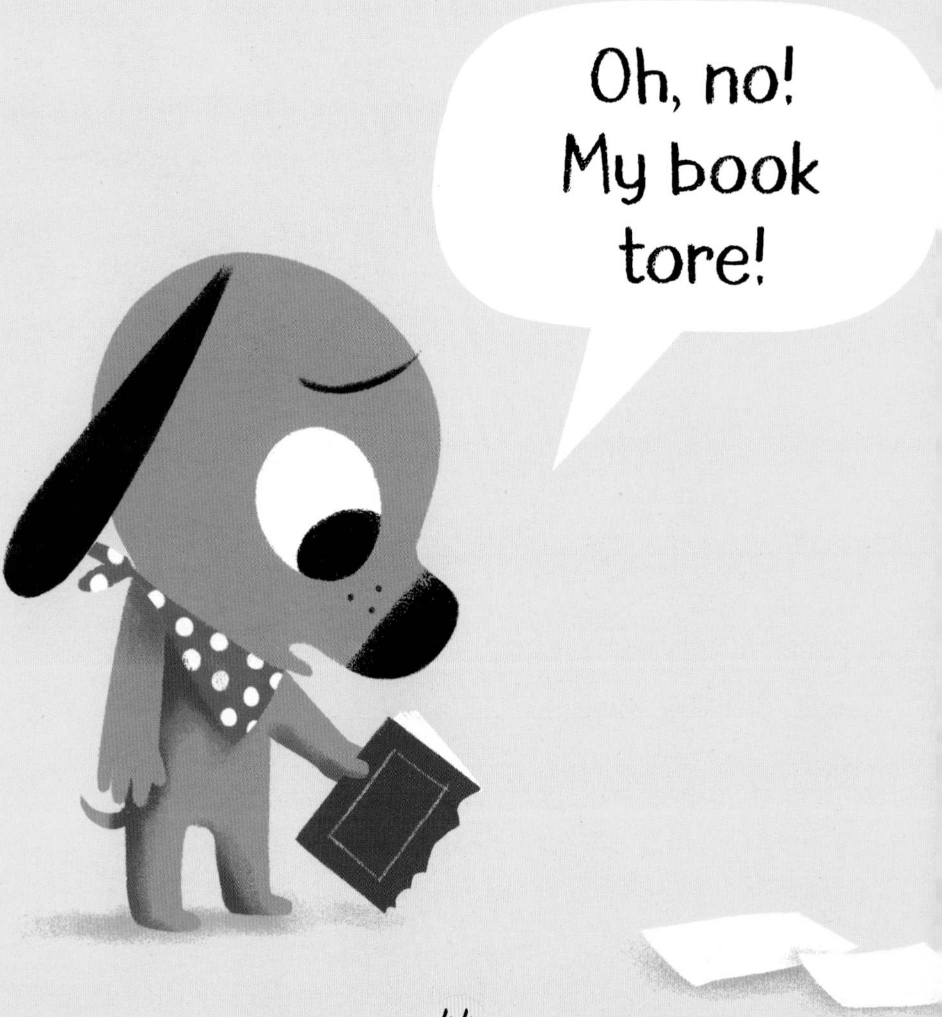
Oh, no!
My book
tore!

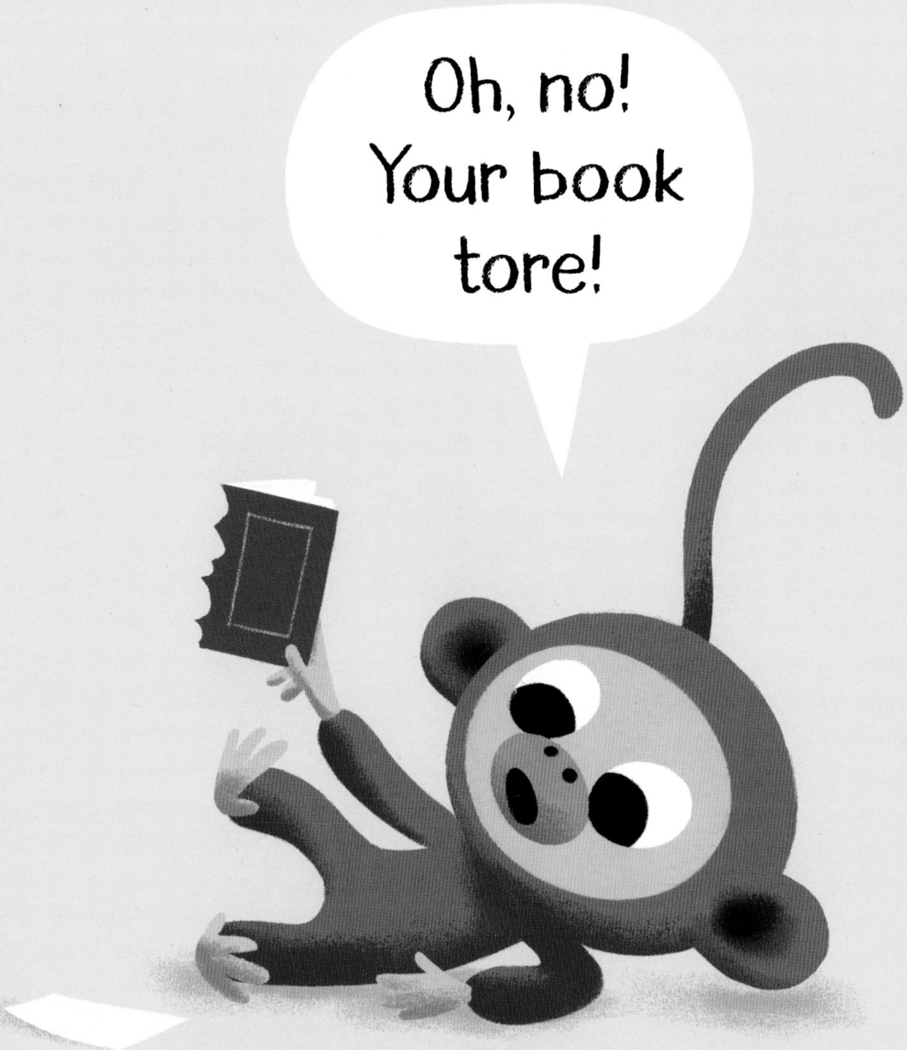
Oh, no! Your book tore!

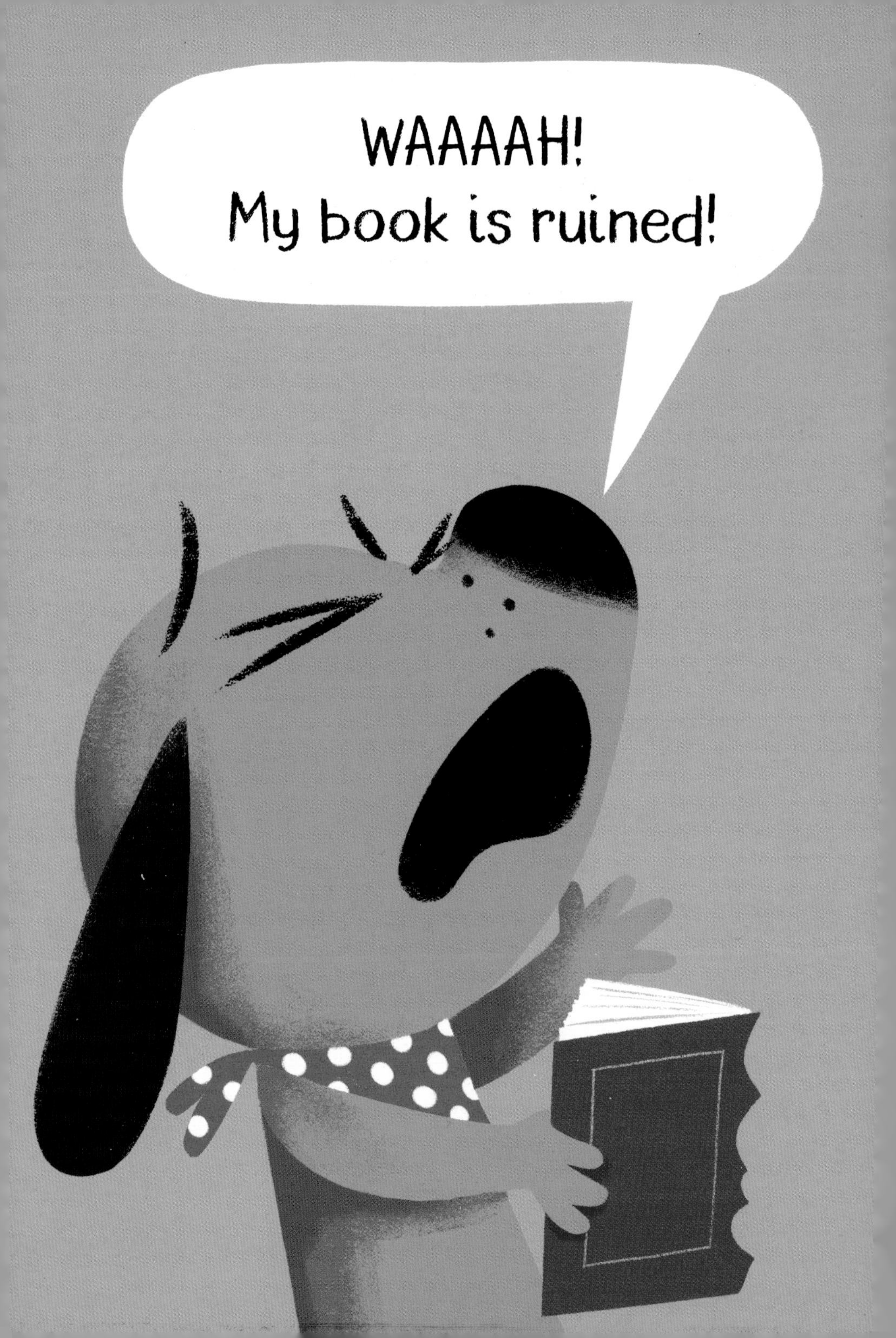
WAAAAH!
My book is ruined!

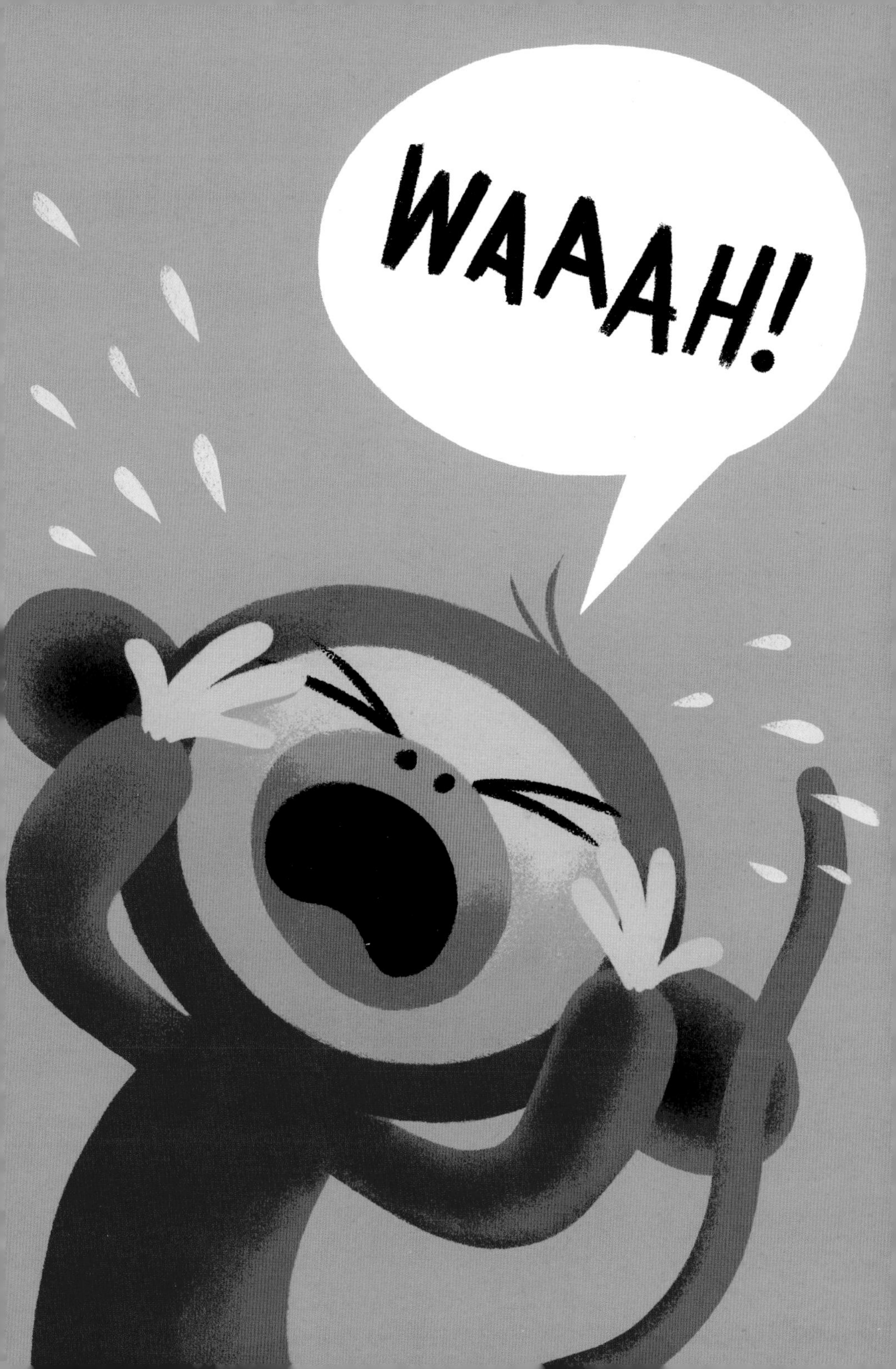
WAAAH!

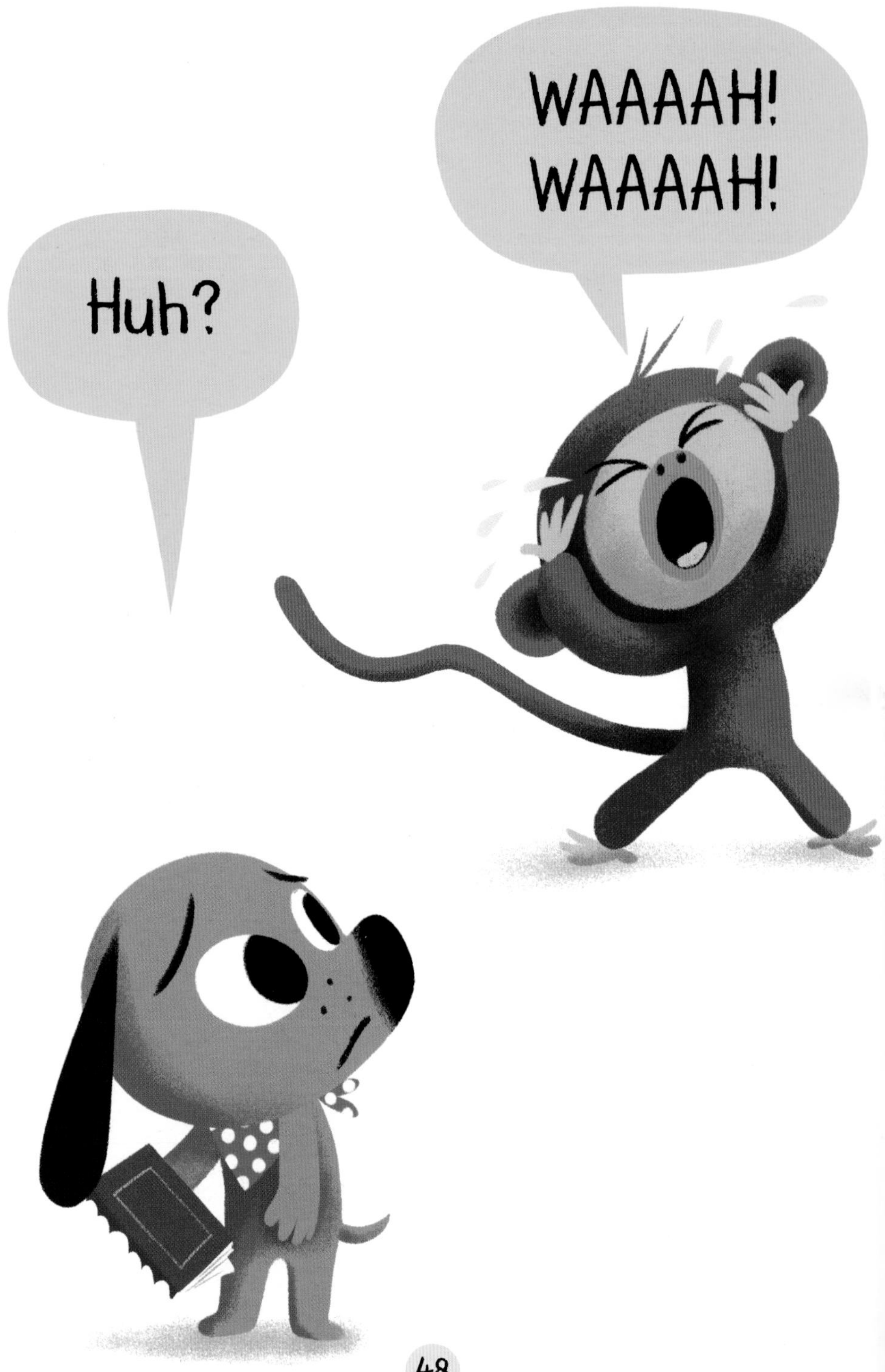
WAAAAH! WAAAAH!
Huh?

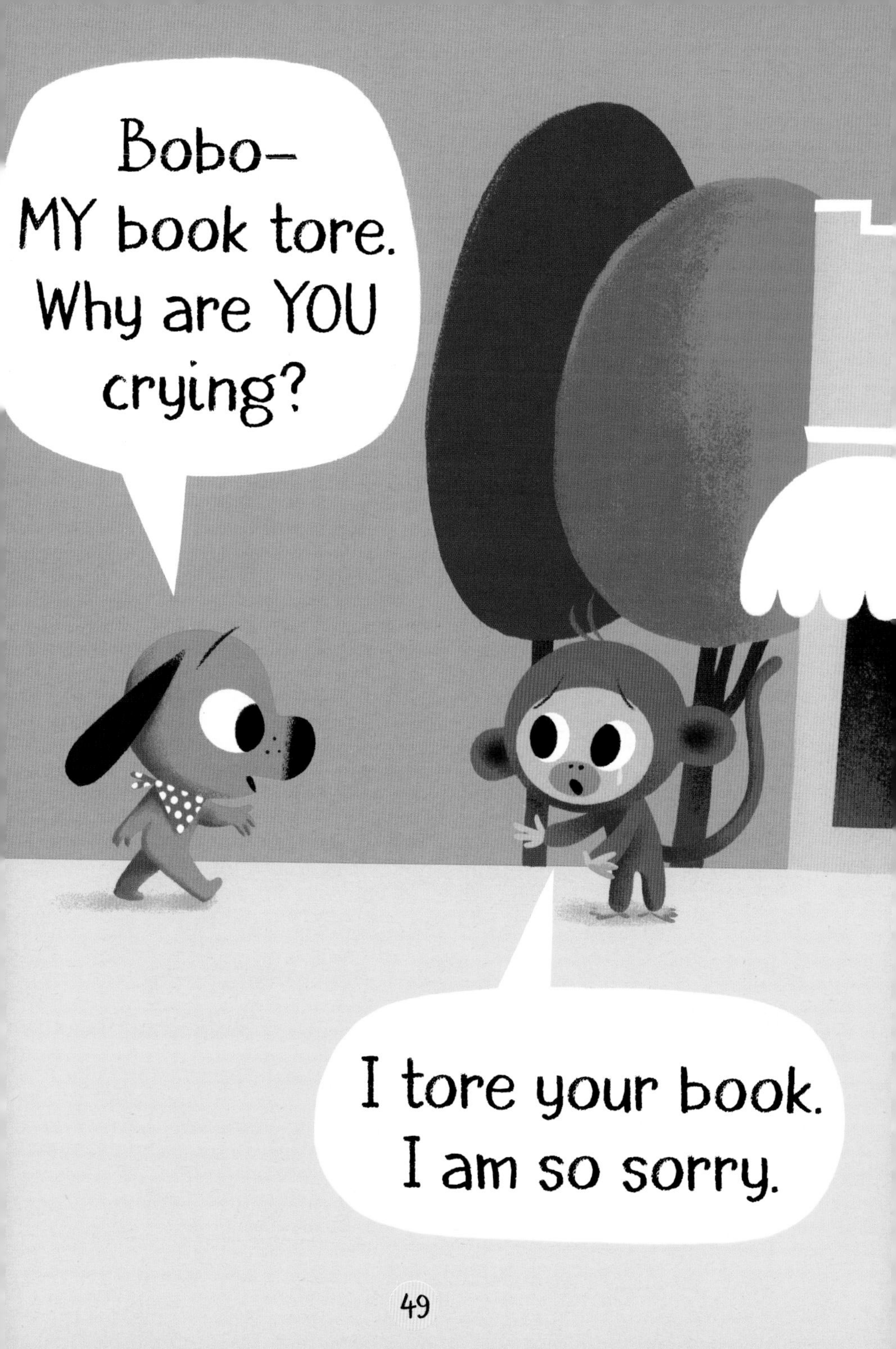
Bobo—
MY book tore.
Why are YOU
crying?
I tore your book.
I am so sorry.

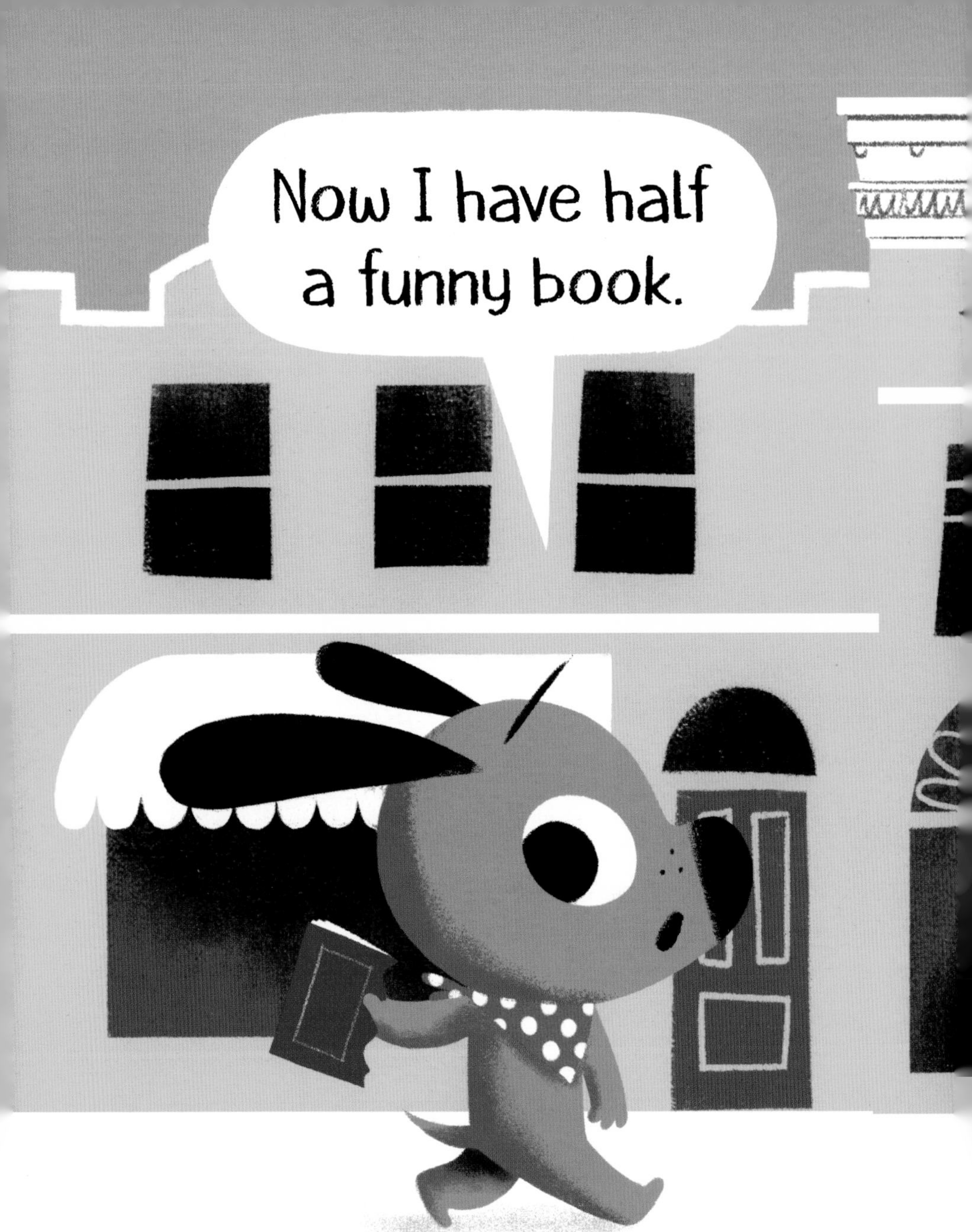
Now I have half
a funny book.

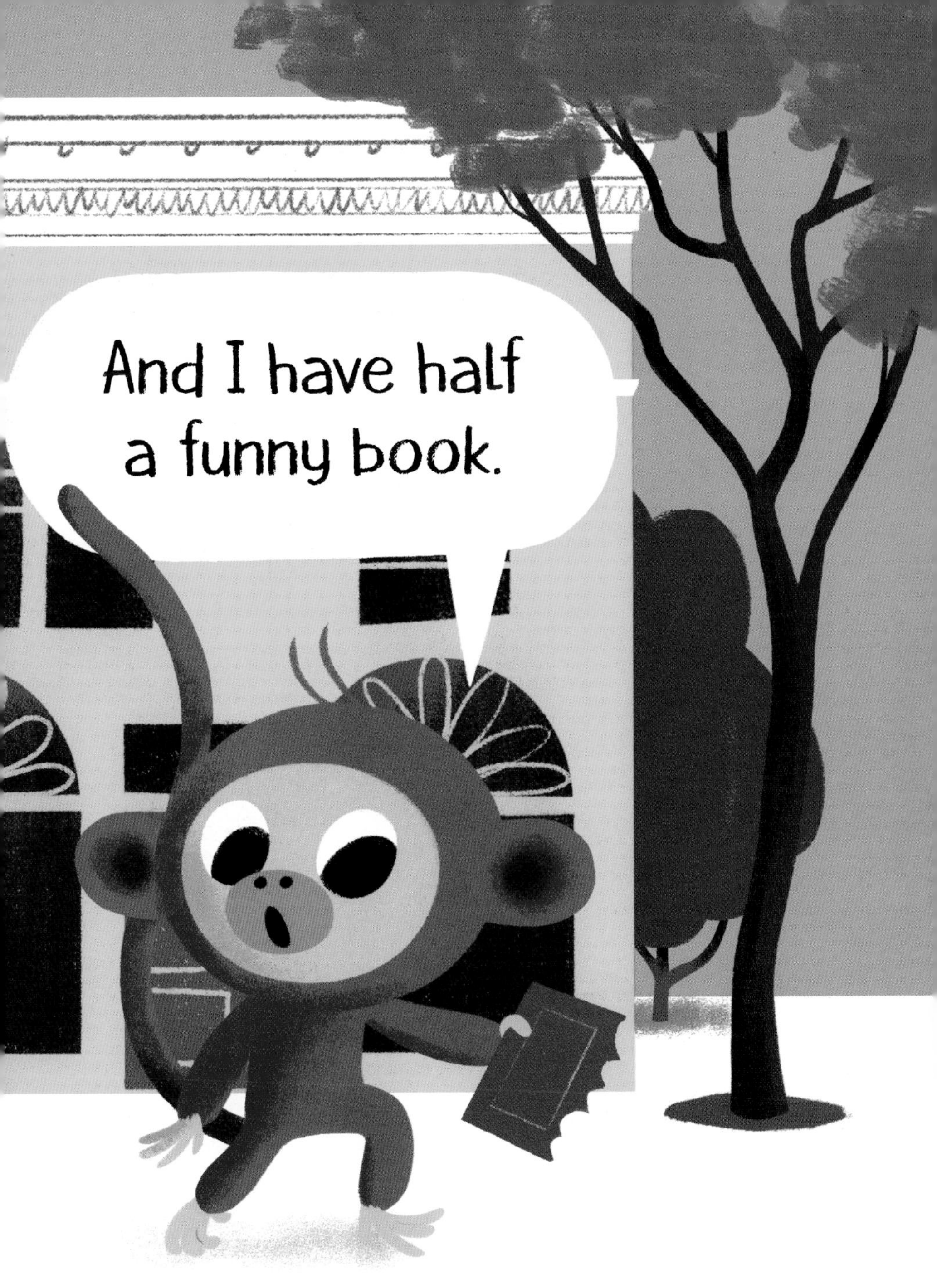
And I have half a funny book.

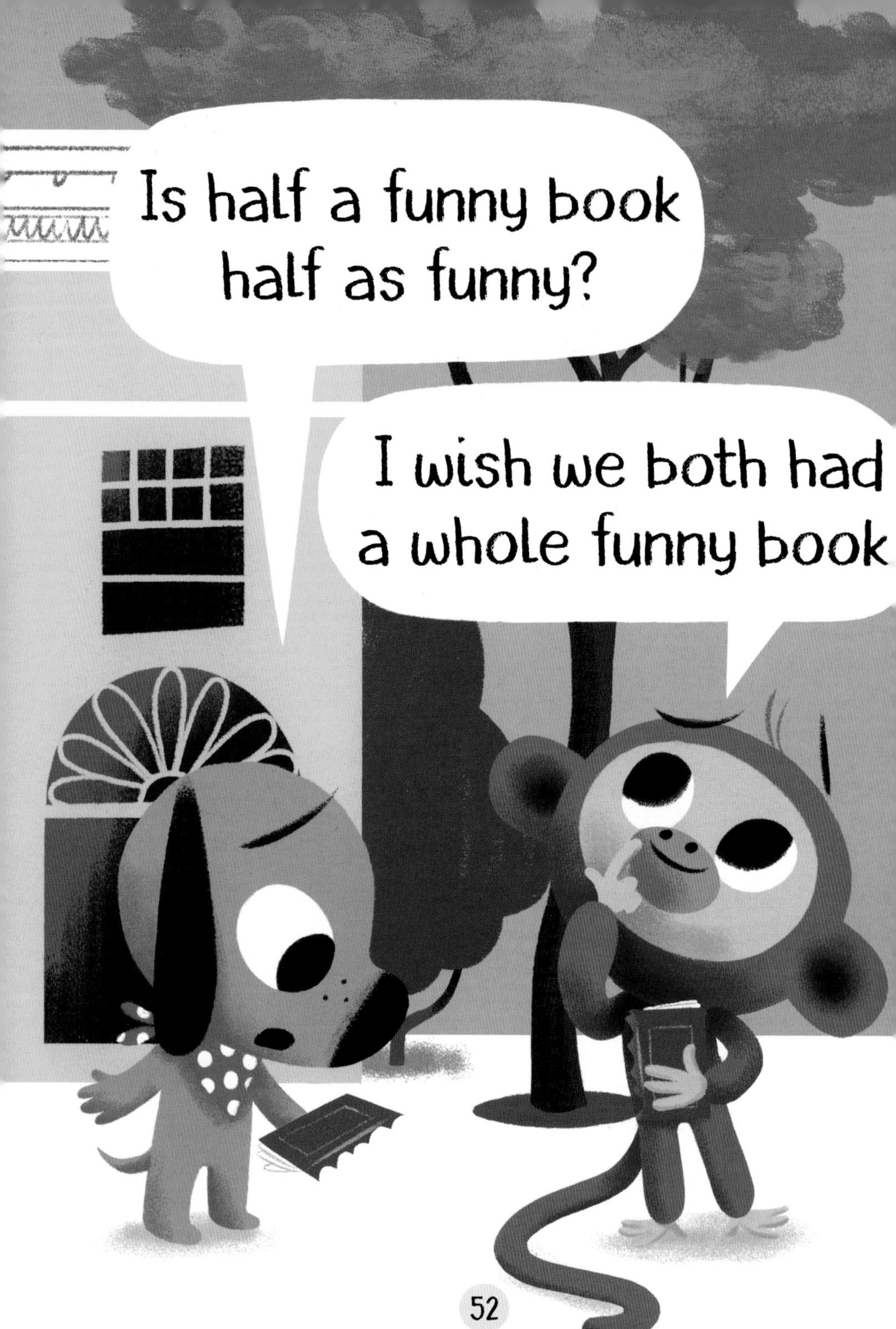
Is half a funny book half as funny?
I wish we both had a whole funny book

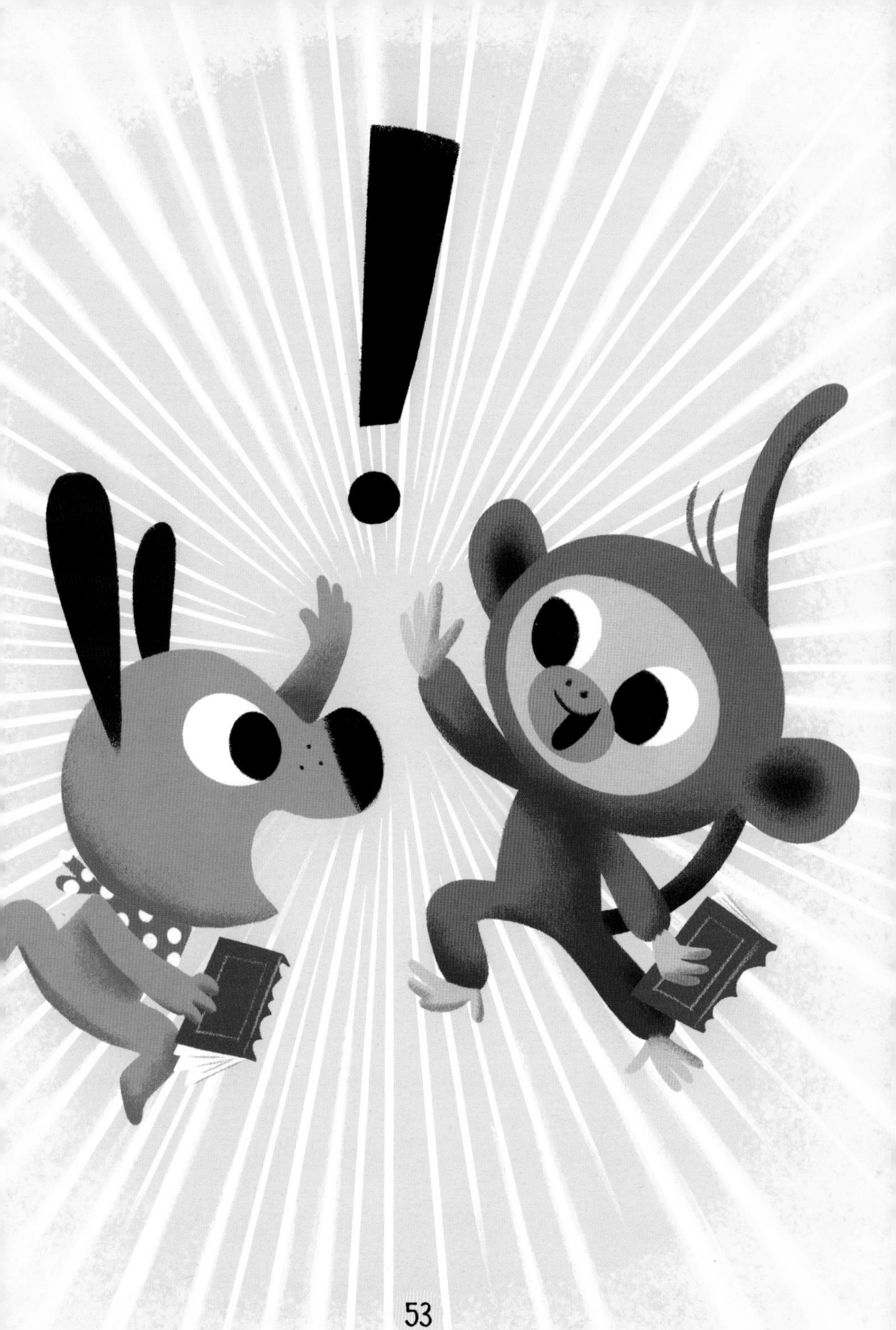
!

Chapter 6
Twice as Funny

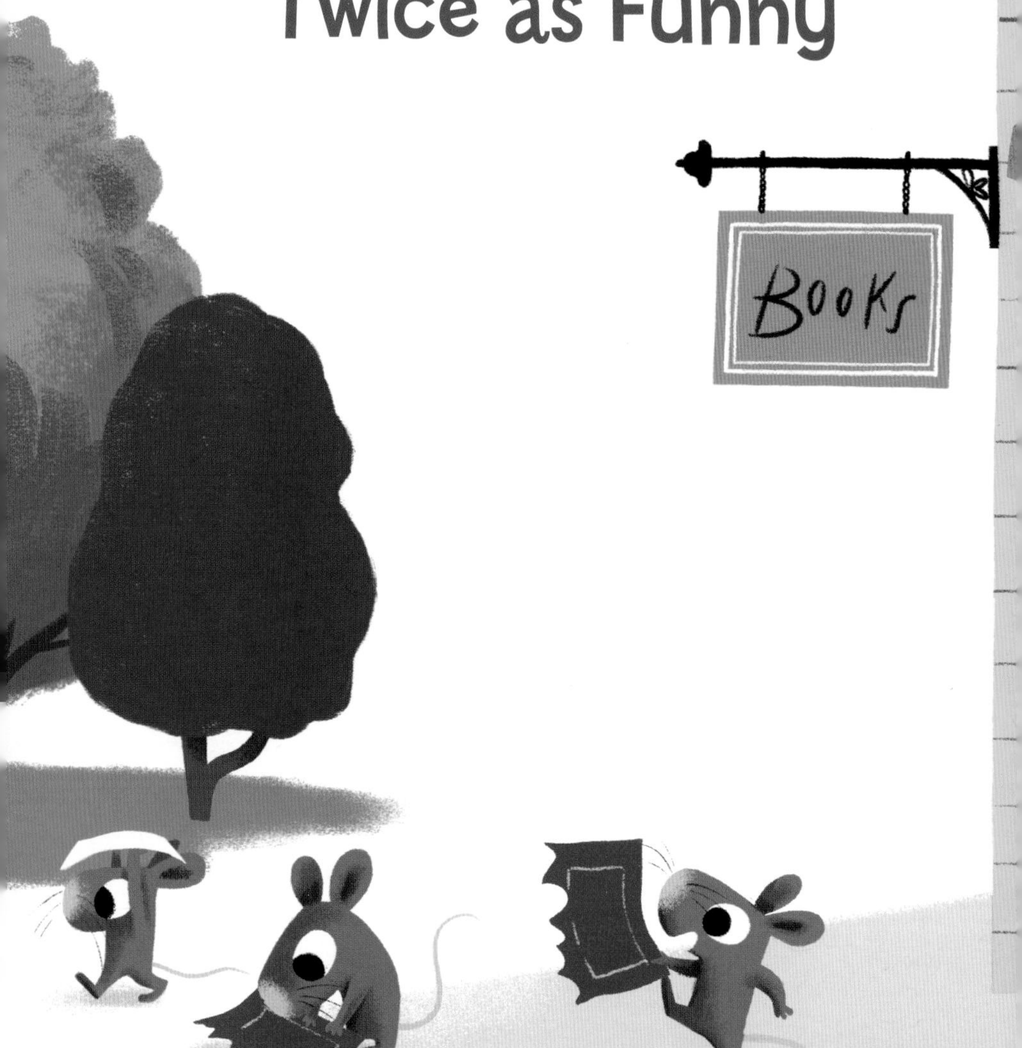
Books

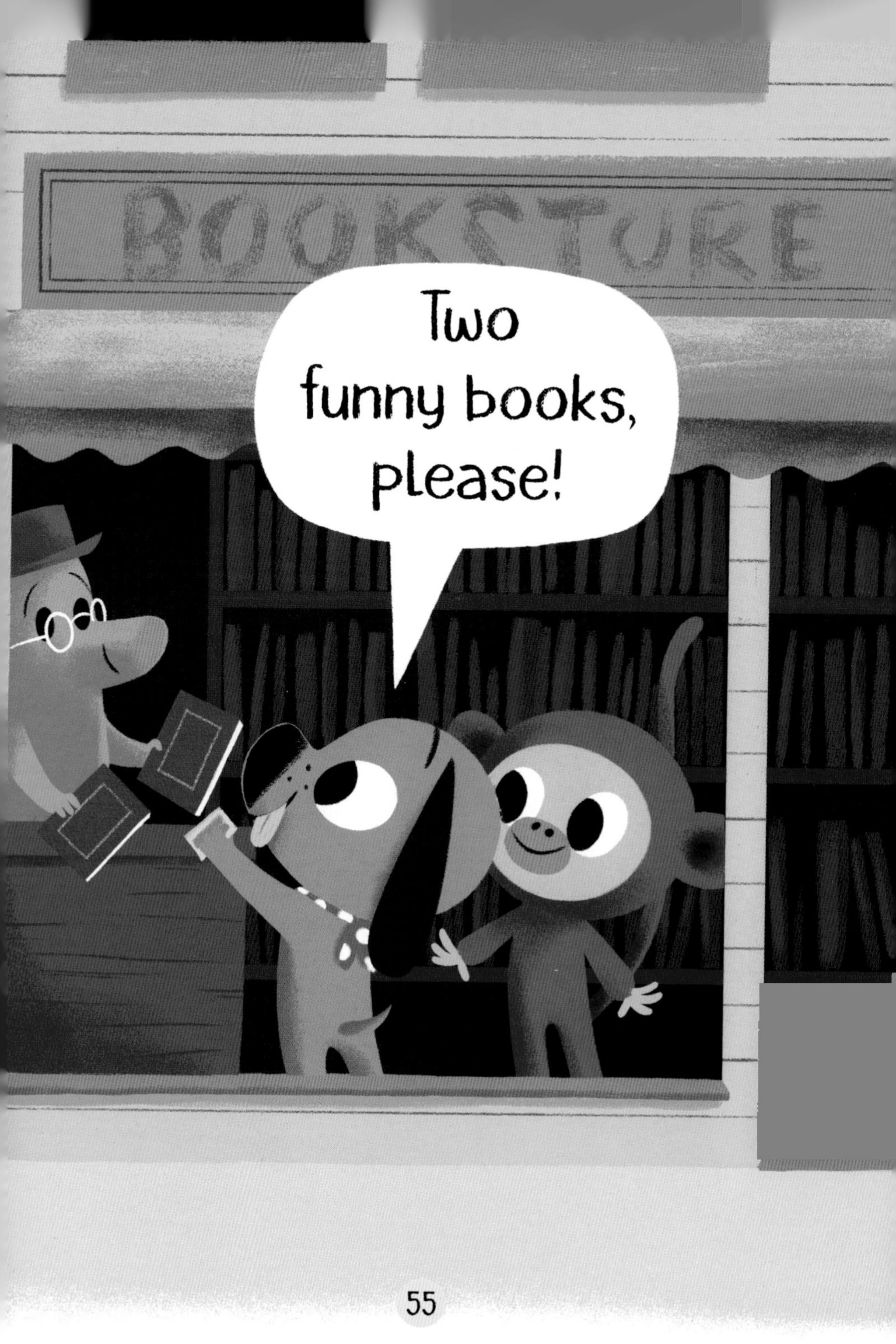
BOOKSTORE
Two funny books, please!

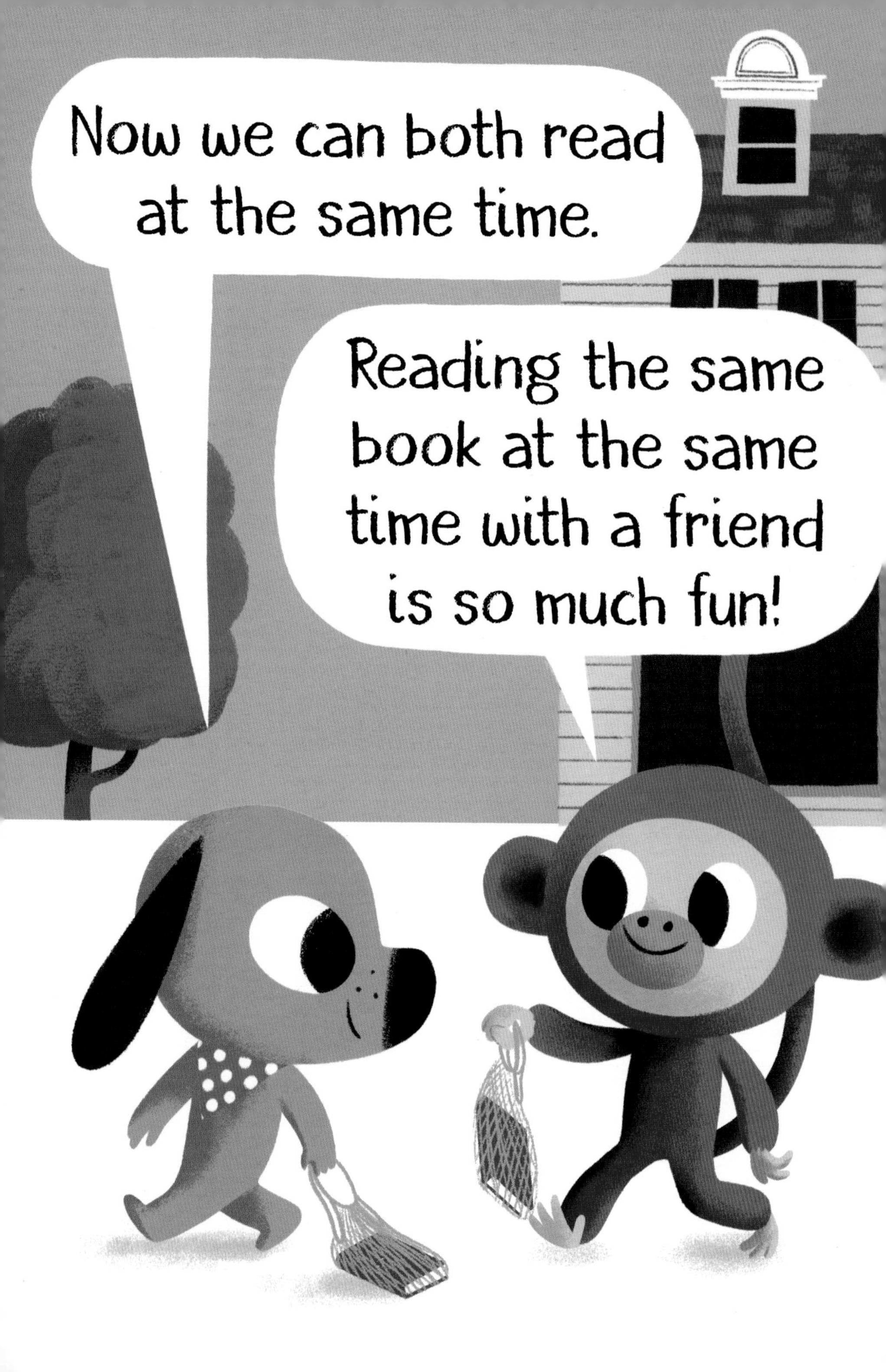
Now we can both read at the same time.
Reading the same book at the same time with a friend is so much fun!

HA! HA!
HEE!
HEE! HEE!

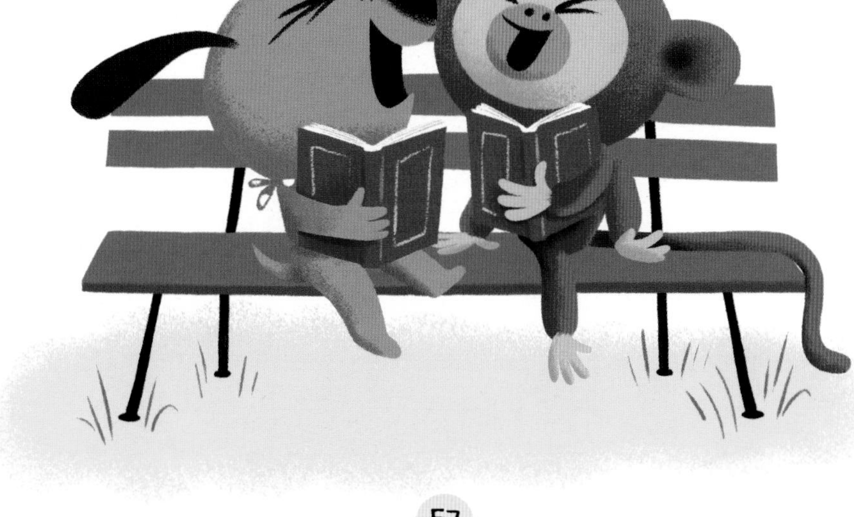

If you liked this FUNNY BOOK, you'll love these!

BOBO and PUP-PUP
WE LOVE BUBBLES!
Vikram Madan • Nicola Slater

BOBO and PUP-PUP
LET'S MAKE CAKE!
Vikram Madan • Nicola Slater

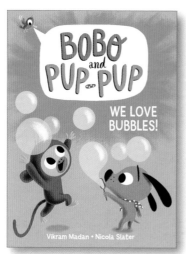

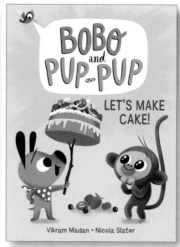

And see what pops up in
Bobo and Pup-Pup's next adventure,
coming in January 2023:

BOBO and PUP-PUP
HATCH AN EGG
Vikram Madan • Nicola Slater

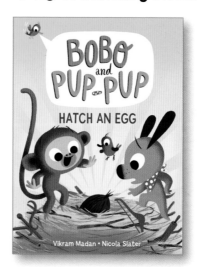

Vikram Madan grew up in India, where he really wanted to be a cartoonist but ended up an engineer. After a long time, he realized that what he really wants to do is make funny books. His self-illustrated book *A Hatful of Dragons: And More Than 13.8 Billion Other Funny Poems* was selected as a Best Book by *Kirkus Reviews*, the New York Public Library, and Bank Street College of Education, among other honors. He lives near Seattle with his family and keeps insisting to them that he should be the one who gets to read every funny book first. Visit him at VikramMadan.com. (And yes, Pup-Pup, half a funny book is only half as funny!)

Nicola Slater lives with her family in the wild and windy north of England. She has illustrated many middle-grade novels and picture books, including *Where Is My Pink Sweater?* (which she also wrote), *Leaping Lemmings!*, *A Skunk in My Bunk!*, and Margaret Wise Brown's *Manners*, a Little Golden Book. In her spare time she likes looking at animals, camping in the rain, and tickling her children. You can follow her on Twitter at @nicolaslater.